Duet

Duet

David Helwig

The Porcupine's Quill

National Library of Canada Cataloguing in Publication

Helwig, David, 1938–
Duet / David Helwig.

ISBN 0-88984-247-7

I. Title.

PS8515.E4D84 2004 C813'.54 C2004-902181-8

1 2 3 4 • 06 05 04

Published by The Porcupine's Quill, www.sentex.net/~pql
68 Main Street, Erin, Ontario NOB 1TO.

Readied for the press by John Metcalf;
copy edited by Doris Cowan.

Represented in Canada by the Literary Press Group.
Trade orders are available from University of Toronto Press.

We acknowledge the support of the Ontario Arts Council, and the Canada Council for the Arts for our publishing program. The financial support of the Government of Canada through the Book Publishing Industry Development Program is also gratefully acknowledged. Thanks, also, to the Government of Ontario through the Ontario Media Development Corporation's Ontario Book Initiative.

To the Saturday Morning Chaps

Carman Deshane put his suitcase on top of the small chest of drawers and went back out to the car. There was a four-lane highway in front of the motel, and behind it a bit of scrubby bush with a creek running through. At the back of his unit was a trailer park. Just along the road, he'd noticed a sign for a planned subdivision. Deshane opened the trunk. Inside was the microwave, an electric kettle, boxes, one with a few dishes and some cutlery. He listened to the sound of a tractor-trailer from the highway. There was a shout from the other side of the square of units. Two guys with an electrician's van, drinking beer, out-of-town tradesmen here for a construction job. He picked up the microwave and walked slowly up the concrete steps from the parking lot and into the motel room. By the time he got to the table next to the front window, he was dizzy, his chest was tight and he was having trouble getting his breath. He put down the shiny black microwave and went and sat on the edge of the bed.

Maybe he should have got someone else to carry it in for him, but he hated to admit to himself that he was that badly off. He imagined his heart, a flabby, weak thing struggling ineffectually to move blood through his body. On the table beside the bed was a bottle of rye. He reached over, took off the cap and took a small swallow. He had pills somewhere in the suitcase, a small pharmacy, the four a day, the two a day, the others, but this was closer.

He put the cap back on the bottle, sat there with it in his hands. First time in his life he'd ever been able to sit still. Now he was too tired to do anything else a lot of the time. His restlessness always drove Audrey crazy. Can't you just sit down for a minute? she'd say, and he couldn't. They'd get in the car and drive somewhere for a coffee, or to a bowling alley in a suburb on the other side of the city, places where he felt like a stranger. Over the years he'd worked most parts of Toronto, and as long as he thought somebody might recognize him as a cop, he couldn't relax. That was why they'd moved to Scarborough, and then farther out after that. Not that it did much good.

When he was working, Deshane liked to be recognized as a cop. They knew who you were, and it kept the shit to a minimum, but it was like a suit of clothes you could never take off. Then he retired and found that without that suit of clothes, he wasn't there at all. His daughter Carol was always suggesting hobbies for him, wood carving or photography. She told him he should write his memoirs. When he first got out of the hospital after the heart attack – six months after Audrey died, six months to the day – he sat down and wrote five pages about joining the navy and going to sea on his first ship, and he carried those pages around with him, though he couldn't have said why, but he knew he was never going to write any more of it.

The day after Audrey's funeral he started to drink, and he stayed drunk for most of a week. When he didn't answer the phone, Carol came and found him, surrounded by mess and empty bottles. He told her he was all right, that he'd get sober and clean it up, and he did. When he had the house back in order, he took a bunch of the old photograph albums round to Carol and Grant, so she could see that he was sober and clean and shaved, and then he went to a real estate agent and put the house on the market.

For almost two years after that he lived in a high-rise apartment, and he hated every day of it. One day he started packing things into the car, dishes, the electric kettle, his winter boots. He didn't know why he was doing it, but it made him feel better. He drove round to see Rolly Menard, his old partner, and they had a drink, a couple of drinks, and just as he was leaving, he asked Rolly if he ever felt as if he wanted to move on, not even knowing where he was going to? Rolly just looked at him and said he was always a weird sucker and clapped him on the back.

After he left Rolly's, he got on Highway 400 and started driving north, and he spent the night in a motel near Huntsville, and he was able to sit with a bottle of rye and watch television without wanting to pitch the bottle through the screen. Now and then he'd go to the front window and see the cars passing. The next morning he drove a few miles along the road and had breakfast in a place with stuffed fish on the walls and old-fashioned wooden booths. He liked that. He stayed three days, and when he got back to the apartment he hated, he decided to move out.

The pain in his chest was better now, and he could breathe more easily. He put the bottle on the bedside table and went back to the car. It was almost dark, and up the hill on the east side of the motel, he could see the lights in a little group of stores. When the stuff was unpacked, he went up to the office at the front. He'd paid a deposit last week when he found the place, and he'd pay a month in advance now while he had the money in his pocket. He'd cashed a pension cheque this morning.

There was a covered walkway that led from the parking lot out to the front of the motel. On one side of the walkway was a door into the office. Inside, there was a young couple renting a room. The man wore a bomber jacket. He had blond hair with a bald spot at the back and short sideburns, a round face that looked hot and red. The girl with him was wearing jeans and a black silk jacket. Her blue eyes – so wide they looked as if she had no eyelids – were glancing around the room trying not to settle on anything while she waited. They'd both been drinking, and the sexual hunger came off the two of them like a smell. The man got the key in his hand, and the two of them were out the door. Behind the counter, the guy who ran the motel was putting away the cash in his wallet. He was slim, good-looking like an old movie star, straight nose, dark eyes, a good mouth, but the skin on his face was slack. He looked over the counter and smiled.

'What can I do for you?'

'I'll pay you the month.'

The man opened a drawer and took out a copy of the receipt for the deposit. He put it on the counter and turned it around.

'Did I ask you your name?'

'Doug,' the man said.

'There you go, Doug.' He put the cash on the counter. There was a sound of laughter from the television set that was playing in Doug's apartment behind the motel office.

'I'll see you later.'

Outside he went back down the walkway and along the path that led to his unit. It was dark now. The couple he'd seen was in one of the units nearby, her legs in the air.

A few minutes later, he was sitting in an imitation English pub, run by a real Englishman. A television set, with the sound off, showed a soccer game. At the bar of the imitation pub sat an imitation cowboy. He wore tight jeans and tooled brown boots, a suede jacket over a denim shirt and a big cowboy hat, and he sat on one of the bar stools with a pint of beer in front of him. He was talking to the bartender, and his voice sounded as if it was produced by something broken. His hands didn't have the look of a man who'd done a lot of hard work with them. Years ago, Audrey took him to a movie about a guy in New York who dressed like that, Jon Voight it was, but he looked to have more fun with the outfit than this guy. Whatever it was this cowboy was waiting for, it was going to be a long wait. Maybe this place was busy on the weekend, but today there were only four people here, Carman, the cowboy and a couple at the table nearest the bar, a pretty redhead and a bulky guy with a moustache. He had thick hands and heavy shoulders, a domed head, balding at the front. His eyes were blood-shot, as if he'd been drinking all day.

The real Englishman came down to his table and Deshane ordered a pint of Guinness. The man dropped a menu in front of him. The guy with the moustache was boasting about how much money he was making from a pyramid sales scheme, and the girl was talking about an agent who might be finding her work in a commercial for Labatt's.

'I have the look they want,' she said.

'Last week,' the cowboy said, 'I was talking to a guy who's looking for extras for a shoot up in Kleinburg.'

Everybody wanted to be in the movies. Even his daughter Carol, who was mostly a sensible girl, got it in her head in high school that she was going to be a model and spent a lot of money on courses for it. The people who made the money were the ones giving the courses. He looked at the cowboy, the awkward face with uneven skin. Instead of getting the train west, you bought the clothes. Soon enough there wouldn't be any trains west, just the little suburban lines taking people from the subdivisions into the city.

'You do have a look,' the cowboy was saying to the redhead. 'A certain kind of thing. A style.' He smiled, hoping to charm, but the smile was awkward on his face.

The redhead smiled back. The man with the moustache had a record – theft, fraud, maybe assault on a woman – he'd bet on it. Deshane looked at the thick hands that lay on the table. He would have liked to go outside and find the man's car – it wouldn't be hard to guess which was his – and put the licence number into the police computer. The redhead looked toward Deshane. He was sure she'd take some rough treatment from the man she was with, but maybe she was happy with that. People got what they wanted. The guy would never have big money to spend on her. For all his talk. Deshane would have liked to put him in jail.

Deshane stood in the open doorway of the motel room and looked at the night sky. Then he got in his car and started to drive. Thousands of headlights moved through the darkness, cars in long lines on their way somewhere. He drove without thinking, found he was on the Don Valley, dodging from lane to lane, and then he was downtown, turning up Parliament then west towards Yonge.

The girl standing at the curb had long shapely legs; the little shorts and high heels showed them off. It was almost a pretty face, toothy and thin. He pulled the car up in front of her, opened the passenger door and waved to her to get in. There was a guy, familiar somehow, in a doorway shouting something at her, but she got into the seat and pulled the door shut behind her.

'You want a blow job?' she said. 'Sixty bucks.'

'I don't know what I want,' he said, but he reached into his wallet as they sat at a red light and took out three twenties and gave them to her. 'Can we take a ride?'

'Are you a cop?' she said.

'Why'd you ask?'

'That guy, Joey, was shouting at me not to go with you, that you were a cop.'

'He your pimp?'

'Thinks he is. Are you a cop?'

'Used to be. I'm retired.'

'You want to fuck me?'

'I don't know. Let's take a ride.'

'You paid. I guess we can do what you want. For a while.'

They were back on the Don Valley, going north.

'Where are we going?'

'Up where I'm staying.'

'You're not, you know, some kind of a pingpong ball, are you?'

'A pingpong ball?'

'Like weird.'

'No. Not about girls anyway.'

'You mean you do boys?'

'I mean I never hurt a woman in my life.'

He wondered if that was true. As the fast lines of cars moved in and out of each other's headlights, he remembered a detective who made a deal with a whore, that he'd let her off on some charge or other if she'd come to his apartment for a little party, just lie there in the bedroom and take on all comers. Deshane had been at the party, and he'd had a couple of drinks and then gone home. It didn't appeal to him. Mostly he'd been faithful to Audrey. When he hadn't, it was once or twice when he was out of town.

The girl in the seat beside him was quiet for a while, then she started to fidget.

'I got to get back to the street, you know.'

'I paid you.'

'How long's it take to give a blow job? We're going to the fucking north pole.'

'A holiday. I'll give you another sixty when we get there.'

'Then I blow you?'

'We'll see.'

'You're taking me to the fucking burbs. I hate the burbs. Fucking Scarberia.'

‘That where you come from?’

‘Fuck, no!’

They drove in silence. He turned off the Don Valley onto the 401.

‘What is this? We going to Montreal?’

He didn’t bother answering. Why couldn’t she just shut up and come along? He’d paid. He’d driven downtown without any plan, and picked her up on impulse, but now, for some reason, he wanted to take her back to the motel. He was stubbornly determined that he was going to do that.

‘You got a cigarette?’

‘I quit. I got a bad heart.’

‘You going to die if you fuck me?’

‘I don’t know. Maybe. Hell of a way to go.’

‘It’d be shit for the girl. Fucking corpse lying on top of you.’

They were pulling into the motel. He drove along the front and turned down the lane that led to the large grassy square at the back, then drove along the edge till he came to his unit. Now that he was here, he was ready to regret the whole thing. It was a stupid idea.

‘Come in and have a drink and I’ll take you back downtown.’

She got out of the car without saying anything and her high heels banged up the steps and across to the door. He opened it, switched on the light and they walked in. Most of the things he’d brought here were still in boxes and the suitcase. He hadn’t bothered to unpack.

‘You live here?’

‘I’m just moving in.’

‘You got a toilet?’

He pointed to the door.

‘I’m ready to piss myself.’

She went off to the bathroom on her high heels, her little ass tilting from side to side under the shorts. He reached into a box, found two glasses and poured some rye into each one. He put hers on the table by the bed and sat down in the chair. He was restless and tired, and his stomach hurt. The girl came back out of the bathroom pulling her shorts straight. He pointed to the glass.

'What's that?'

'Whisky.'

'I don't drink whisky.'

'So leave it.'

But she picked up the glass and took a swallow.

'You going to ask how a nice girl like me got to be a whore?'

'Because you're too lazy and stupid to do anything else.'

'Fucking cheap shot.'

She drank more whisky.

'You want to see my tits?'

'Sure.'

The shirt she was wearing was pink, with a pattern of silver sequins. She pulled it up and he looked at her breasts, small and young and raw, one bigger than the other.

'You don't have a wife?' she said as she put the shirt back down.

'She's dead.'

'You fucked anybody since then?'

'No.'

'Think you still can?'

He didn't answer. He could feel the pressure in his shoulders and back, and the beginning of the pain. He got up and went to the suitcase, got out a pill and put it under his tongue, felt the burning sensation against the membrane. Then he went back to the chair.

'Listen, if you're going to die or something. I'm getting the fuck out of here, and you still owe me some money.'

He took his wallet out of his jacket pocket and held some bills out to her. She took them and put them in the pocket of her shorts.

'You want me to do something?'

'I'll be OK in a minute.'

He listened to the sound of his own breathing, a car starting up in the parking lot, the hum of traffic on the highway, the sound of the girl tapping her fingernails against the glass of whisky. He breathed slowly. The girl's face was tense and ugly, the lips drawn back over the teeth as if she might start to bite and scratch.

It was taking a long time for the pain and pressure in his chest to ease. He might need another pill. He closed his eyes and waited, concentrating on sounds, on the hum of cars on the highway.

'I got to get out of here,' the girl said.

He couldn't open his eyes. All he could do was to concentrate on breathing, on staying alive. He thought he heard the sound of the door. He waited, and very slowly he started to feel a little better.

When he opened his eyes, the girl was gone. He went to the door to see if she was waiting for him by the car, but there was no sign of her. Well, she had enough of his money. He locked the door behind him, got undressed and got into the bed.

Norma was imagining elevators. Her legs had been bad for a couple of days, and getting back and forth between the store and her apartment above wasn't easy. Sitting in her rocking chair, she was reflecting on the wonderful small elevator that could be installed to carry her like some stage divinity from earth to the realms above. She couldn't afford such a thing, of course, and would not be able to between now and the final apotheosis (or mere dropping dead), but there was a certain pleasure in looking across the store and seeing the imaginary elevator rising, like a vast dumb waiter, herself seated in it, a complacent smile on her face.

Norma was surrounded by things for sale that mostly no one bought, or so it seemed. She tried to calculate whether business was altogether bad or if this was a mood. Moods, the weather of heart and soul. She was ready to face the blizzards, the hurricanes and snowstorms, but not days of cloud. Cloud today. No blaming the menopause, which was safely past.

She needed to do something. No point sitting here being A Victim of Circumstance. This was what she had chosen, and now she must go on choosing it. Vacationers were arriving at the nearby lakes, and some of the things for sale would actually be sold.

By the back stairs, on a bedside table painted purple, was a portable tape player along with an assortment of tapes she'd picked up from a couple who wanted to sell a garage full of stuff when they moved. They put the damnedest things on tape nowadays. She got up, went to it, and put on her favourite, the one of tropical bird calls, and there she was among exotic trees, green air, green earth and warmth that went all the way into her sore bones. A foreign land with a foreign sun, deep comfort to the soul and body.

She was at the back of the store, where it hung over the ravine, looking always a little in danger of tumbling in, and she could see the sun in the leaves of one of the large maples that also hung over the rock cliff. At her feet was the narrow wooden staircase that led down to a small storage room with one tiny window and cracks in the floor opening into empty space. There was a trap door over the stairwell, and she kept it closed in winter; to be in the little room was as cold as being outside. Its side walls appeared to be hanging from a few nails in the floor joists, which were cantilevered over the ravine.

The tape ended with a loud click. She went down the stairs, which were steep, and as she went, she held on to things, floor, wall, to balance herself. On the darkest days she imagined coming down here, pulling the trap door shut behind her and waiting for death or some other revelation to visit her. If she was alone, let her be alone. Once there was a husband. Once. Company. A vain, foolish man, but weren't they all? Open their zippers and their brains fall out. She couldn't remember if she'd heard that or made it up, but she'd used it a lot. And her tough story about going to see Steven and his bimbo, crashing into the house and pulling the sheet off the poor bare creature. It made a good story, and at first she had thought it was funny, when she was wild and crazed and out of control, but for years afterward she remembered the girl's body, the patch of pubic hair bigger and longer and thicker than hers had ever been, a forest where things happened that gave them joy, while Norma lay alone and chilled.

She didn't know where they were any more, or if they were together, and when she saw her son Arthur she didn't ask. Arthur found her eccentric and tried to avoid her.

Norma turned in a circle. Why? Because. Why was she down here? Because. She turned again. There was some child's game where you turned like that. Or they spun you to make you dizzy. She turned once more, then three more times. Norma has turned six times in a circle, now what will she see? A little dizzy, she leaned against the wall beside the window. To the right was the trunk of a maple tree, rising at an angle from the soil at the side of her neighbours' house. It looked as if the roots went under the house and might lift the foundation if the tree should fall, and they talked of having it cut down. Imagine it tilting into the ravine, the corner of the house lifting, cracking. Sometimes she liked visions of disaster, the floorboards cracking beneath her, her fat old body plunging down onto the rocks.

She listened to the waterfall. In the ravine, sunlight glittered on the racing water. Short-sighted, her glasses left upstairs, she could see no details, only a pattern of grey and silver and green and black, and those flashes of light, and then another moment of dizziness spun her brain, and she had to lean back and close her eyes.

When she opened them again, she was staring at the stone wall that made one side of the little room and supported the framework of the building above. Against it were piled two or three boxes of books left here until she had time to sort and price them. Beside them an old school desk, the writing surface missing. Her business was rescue, of the abandoned, the fragmentary, the useless; her business was faith in unlikely possibilities. She was like the therapists, all those lullaby boys, who found the little fragments of strength and hope, and listened, their listening a song of comfort, those miners of darkness, those lullaby boys, but her work of salvage had its own dignity. Who would ever find a place for that broken school desk, stitch it back into the fabric of life? Not without its comic nobility, this garbage-picking business of hers. Save us all, Norma, the broken things cry out. Oh save us from the landfill site, from burial and rot, for we have the beauty of manufacture upon us. We were produced by the wilful brain and would not return to being mere atoms. Save us, Norma, save us.

She turned herself around in a circle once more, she couldn't resist it, and she promised all the lost objects of the world that she would do her best to save them.

And then she was sitting on the floor of the little storeroom and she was cold. It must have been all that foolish spinning that brought her down, and now she was wakening from some kind of doze, and chilled through. Cool air rose from the earth and rocks through the gaps in the floorboards. Even the sound of the waterfall was cold. She wondered if she could summon the strength to stand up; there were whole days now when weakness took her in this powerful impersonal way, and she was only aware of her incapacity in its grip.

She tried to get up, had to turn round on hands and knees, sunlight there below on grey and green shapes, something blue. Got hold of an old board nailed across the studs and heaved herself up, on her feet now, leaning against the wall and panting. Down here so long, there must be something to be found, some message. She walked slowly across the room to a pile of cartons. On top of one was a small cigar box. Norma couldn't remember ever seeing it; it must have arrived with a truckload. She lifted the lid.

Even in the dim corner of the room there was a glint of light, and when she took the box toward the window, a reflection of full daylight fell on the shards of pale shining gold, with patches of darker colour, sharp lines of fracture on the surface. She reached into the box and took one of the shiny pieces of material in her fingers. It was light as a sheet of paper. A tiny fragment broke off, split into even thinner sheets.

It was years since she had walked through the woods to one of the old mica mines. They were derelict now, dangerous water-filled holes surrounded by second growth bush. In the early days of settlement, farmers hauled wagonloads of the golden ore into the larger towns to sell, a cash crop that could be harvested in winter.

A thin layer of mica slid loose under the pressure of her fingers. Clear as glass or the water in a forest pool, the pale brown of water over fallen leaves. She held it to the light and saw the world golden beyond it.

He woke in the dark, and he felt a great happiness, and then he knew that he had been dreaming of Audrey, that in the dream she was alive and they were together, but the dream was over, and the room was black and cold, and he wanted to be asleep again, but he knew that he would lie awake now, listening to his heart beat. He tried to remember the dream, as if that might bring some comfort, but every second it was farther from him, and the memory was a taunting of his solitude.

He pulled himself up in bed and turned on the light on the bedside table. There was a book open there, a science fiction paperback he'd bought at the milk store when he went there to get instant coffee. It was one of those stories about the development of dangerous new germs, and it kept him reading. Beside it stood the bottle of rye and a small glass. He poured just a little of the amber whisky into the glass, picked up the book, and started to read, taking a little sip now and then. It was better than lying in the dark hoping for sleep to come.

This was how you passed the night. He looked up from the book and examined the room. The wall facing him was made of concrete blocks, heavily painted. One course of blocks and beyond that there was another identical room, empty, or with a stranger lying asleep. It was very quiet. If he listened carefully, he might hear a car or truck passing on the highway. The curtains that he'd drawn over the window had a pattern of running deer. Over the foot of the bed was a cheap blue blanket with a lot of the colour worn out of it.

It reminded him of a motel room that he and Audrey had rented in Florida, near Fort Myers. How they spent hours walking on the beach and always tracked sand into the room. The salt fishy stink of the shells Audrey collected and brought back to the room was all around them as they lay close together on the bed. It was an ordinary sort of place, but it was their best holiday, one of the times he'd forgotten about Toronto.

Even as he sat there, perfectly still in bed, he could feel the chaos in his chest as the ruined heart laboured to do its work. The doctor would listen to the heart and test his blood pressure and find more pills to prescribe to keep him alive for a few more days, a few more weeks. He already had the blue ones, the yellow ones, and the black and yellow capsules to put under the tongue. Not much point to it all, but something in you didn't let you quit.

It was hard to live without work. What you did. How you spent your life. You complained about it, but there was nothing else really. He hadn't been trained for this emptiness. Starting in the navy, tossing around in a corvette in the North Atlantic, there were jobs to be done. The decks awash in rough weather, other ships, friendly and hostile invisible in the rain and fog, and in the worst of it you slept where and when you could and woke for your watch and hoped to survive. Now you were useless. It was unfair of Audrey to have died. To have left him like this. Mostly women lived longer, and they were better at it, somehow, just living.

He took another sip of whisky and tried to go back to reading about the killer germs attacking the city. It was how you passed the night.

Sometimes Norma gave up on sleep. She would get up and read or wander around the store, or even go out for a walk, and after an hour or so, go back to bed. It was easier to sleep once it began to be light. Tonight, she'd lain awake for an hour, and now she was making her way, a little laboriously, down the steps to the store. She would sit there in her rocking chair for a while and stare out into the night, as if she were thinking. Or maybe she would be thinking. Sometimes she wasn't altogether sure what thinking was; apparently there were those who could do it in a step-by-step sequential way, whose brains set up and solved equations with no irrelevant interference from daydreams and bodily needs and scraps of old memories.

Maybe she didn't have anything large enough to think about. She went step by step down to the store, a dressing gown over her cotton pyjamas, silly childish things like those track suits that people wore to go bouncing by her windows. Norma remembered a time when it would have been inconceivable for respectable men and even more for respectable women to run up and down the streets in odd collections of clothing. That was something to think about, as she sat there in her rocking chair, why all that had changed.

Why do things change? Now there was a subject for meditation. She could have a good long rock over that one. She reached the bottom of the stairs, twisted her hip the wrong way, flinched from pain, and went to the front window. To survey the empty night street. There were streetlights on this part of the main street, though it wasn't clear why. No one walked out there at this hour.

Except someone was.

A child standing in the street, looking toward the old hotel which stood empty and ominous a few feet away on the other bank of the narrow river. She unlocked the door and went out to the sidewalk. The small figure looked in her direction, interested but also unconcerned. It was the boy from the cottage she rented out, son of the young woman from Virginia who'd turned up a few days ago.

'I'm Luke,' he said.

'What are you doing out in the middle of the night?'

'Exploring.'

'Shouldn't you be in bed?'

'I don't know.'

'Of course you know. And you should. Your T-shirt's on backwards.'

'It was dark when I was gettin' dressed.'

Norma liked his Virginia accent. He looked perfectly self-possessed as he stood there in the street, but she couldn't just leave him, not at this hour.

'Do you want to come in here?' she said.

'No. I want to go in there.' He was pointing to the hotel.

'Why?'

'I don't know.'

'At night?'

'Sure.'

'Aren't you scared?'

'I wouldn't be if you came with me.'

That shut her up. Here she was in her pyjamas and nightgown, at some unknown hour of the morning, on the main street of the village, talking to a small child, who was, in his innocent way, propositioning her.

'Come in before we wake up the whole neighbourhood,' she said.

They entered the store, and Norma closed the door behind them.

'Actually I need to pee,' he said.

'Children always need to pee,' she said. 'It's one of the things I remember about children. They always need to pee but especially when you're in a car on a busy highway.'

'Do you have children?'

'I have one boy, grown up. His name is Arthur.'

Unseen for some time now. Probably as a result of her own foolishness, which was endless.

'Why didn't you pee on the side of the road in the bushes. People do that in the country.'

'I forgot.'

'Well, the toilet's upstairs. I'll show you.' She started back up the stairs, weary by the time she was halfway, but trying not to show it.'

'Does it hurt you to climb up the stairs?'

'How did you know that?'

'I don't know.'

'An old cripple eh?'

He didn't say anything. He was too young for polite reassurance, probably didn't know it was being asked for. Upstairs she turned on lights, wondering if the boy saw the place as a mess. Or maybe he was used to such things. She pointed out the toilet, and while he was in there, she went to her bedroom and pulled on pants and a shirt over her pyjamas, put on a pair of sandals. When she came back out, the boy was standing in the kitchen.

'You got dressed,' he said.

'Well, you're dressed. Did I put my shirt on backwards?'

'I can't tell.'

'Neither can I.'

'Are we going to see that place?'

'You mean the hotel?'

'Is that what it is?'

'It's what it used to be.'

'It doesn't look like a hotel.'

'Not like a hotel in a big city. This is just a small village and that's an old-fashioned hotel, but that's what it is.'

'I stayed in a hotel once when I was little.'

'Where was that?'

'New York. My mom's boyfriend took us there. Matt. He used to be her boyfriend. He used to make her cry.'

The boy's face was sweet and blank. What did he see in hers?

'So you want to look at the hotel,' she said.

'I thought it was a haunted house.'

'Have you ever seen a ghost?'

'No.'

She opened a closet where she thought there was a large flashlight.

'We'll go and take a look,' she said, 'if I can find the flashlight. I don't think we better go inside tonight. It would be too dangerous. We could fall through a hole in the floor or the stairs might collapse.'

'That would be neat.'

'No, it wouldn't. We'd get hurt. But we can have a look around, and if you stay a while, I'll try and get hold of the people that own it and see if I can show you inside some day. I'll tell them you want to buy it.'

'I don't have enough money.'

'I won't tell them that. And don't you tell them that either.'

'OK.'

'Do you know my name?' She couldn't find the flashlight, was opening drawers now.

'No.'

'Norma.'

'OK.'

'That's OK is it?'

'Sure.'

She had finally found the flashlight, in the cupboard under the sink. Like as not the batteries would be dead. She pressed the button forward and the light came on.

'Good,' the boy said, with that placid male sense that his approval mattered. There were worse ways to be, she supposed, than feeling that the world was significantly the better for your satisfaction with it.

'And after we look at the hotel, you'll go back to the cottage and get to bed?'

He nodded, and they started down the stairs. The hotel was one indication of the generally lousy state of property values in the village. The last Norma heard, it was owned by a family in Toronto who had inherited it from the son of the last man to run it, and they were waiting for the price to go up before they tried to sell it. Standing there by the river through winter wind and summer sun, the paint was peeling, and the wood, good old white pine as it was, deteriorating. The day would come when there was nothing to do but tear it down.

She and the boy stood in the street and looked at the frame building. There were two small balconies on the second floor, one overlooking the street, and one built over the ravine, looking toward the brick wall of Norma's store, the wall with the faded advertisement for boot polish, ghostly now, old-fashioned type, old-fashioned words.

Sometimes at night she thought she heard voices from that balcony, voices singing.

The windows in the front were boarded up, and there was a sheet of plywood over the front door, but she remembered that there was a window along the far side that they could peek in. She led the boy down that side.

'Be careful,' she said. 'You could break your leg.'

'So could you,' he said.

'I know.'

She played the light on the ground in front of her, ground which was full of weeds and stones and tough springy Manitoba maples. She pushed past a couple of them, whipped by twigs, and looked back to see how Luke was doing. He slid neatly through and stood close to her. The window was a few feet ahead. It wasn't boarded, but the earth sloped down so it was just above her head.

'The window's too high to see in,' she said.

'You could lift me.'

'Could I?'

'Sure.'

Ahead of them to the left and a little below, she could see a light through a black lace of leaves. A window in one of the houses along the river. Earlier there had been a bit of wind, but now it was still. There was something. In the distance.

'Listen,' she said.

They listened. A breath of air, the rattle of old leaves and then the almost silence. A sound, faint and far off.

'What is it?' he said.

'Wolves,' she said. 'Wolves howling. But a long way from here.'

'Really wolves?'

'Really.'

They listened again. The sound drifted away. You thought you heard it, but you knew now you were probably imagining it.

'There are really wolves here?' he said.

'Near here.'

'I didn't know that,' he said, appreciative.

Norma stood closer to the window. She shone her light up into the room and saw the grooves of a wooden ceiling. This old place could be quite something, with a few thousand dollars and a little imagination. Well, quite a few thousand dollars and a lot of imagination.

'Are you going to lift me?' he said.

'I'll try. Then that's it for tonight. You go home to bed.'

He came over close to the window. She gave him the flashlight and tried to decide how to lift, bent her knees and put her arms around his legs and did her best to stand up. She gasped. There were pains all up and down her back, but she got him up to where his head was even with the glass of the window. He put his arms up to shine the flashlight in the window and looked intently.

'What's it like?'

'It's empty, but it's funny. It's like a picture in a book.'

'I can't hold you any longer.'

Trying to bend to put him down, she lost her footing, tumbled, and found herself lying on the ground, with a sore hip where she'd fallen against the edge of a rock. The boy stood with the flashlight in his hand, waiting for her to get up. She managed to do it, not gracefully, but she was on her pins again, though a bit dizzy and wobbly.

'Well, this is quite an adventure.'

'Yes, it is,' he said.

He handed her the flashlight, and they made their way back to the front of the hotel. She half expected to meet police or a suspicious neighbour, but the street was empty up to the curve both ways. There was a little puff of wind against her face, and the waterfall went on with its endless idiotic roar.

Carman Deshane had no idea where he was. Yesterday he started to drive north then east. Last night he'd found a motel on Highway 7, and in the morning he started out again, taking back roads, making turns on impulse, and now he was in the middle of nowhere. The road he'd been following had come out of a stretch of woods and past a small house, not much more than a shack, that stood helplessly on the rock that cropped up everywhere here, and then the road ended where it met another at right angles. So he turned right on the new road and it was leading him through a marsh, the water lapping against the sides, coming almost over the roadway itself. At low points, the ruts were full of water and he couldn't see past the thick growth of reeds. Water splashed up and he half expected the engine to stall, the car to coast to a slow stop.

He wondered how many miles it was back to the little frame house. There had been a skinny old man in black rubber boots standing in the yard, staring at his car as it passed by. A pile of split wood beside him and a rickety sawbuck beside that. The wreck of a car rusting away at the edge of the woods behind the house. Then it was gone and he'd found himself on this dirt road that looked as if it might vanish into the long reaches of the marsh. Ahead of him the road dipped and was completely covered by water. It wasn't clear how deep the water was, and he could see the car going in, sinking down, vanishing. Miles of country out here without a single human being in it. It had been settled and logged a long time ago, and now most of those who had settled it had abandoned it for an easier life.

Water sprayed up the sides of the car, but he came out the other side and the road began to bend to the right and he saw a small hill where it vanished into another patch of woodland. As he drove up the slope into the trees, he noticed that there wasn't much gas left in the car. If he saw a sign anywhere for a town, he'd better follow it. Otherwise he'd find himself out of gas at the side of one of these meaningless old roads. He didn't have it in him to walk for miles, and he had no idea how long it would be before another car appeared.

It was a cloudy day. The depths of the woods were secretive and still. He could stop the car, wander off into the trees, lie down to die like an old dog, curled in a hollow among the fragrant piles of leaf-mould.

A few miles further on, there was a crossroads and a little sign with the name of a town, and beyond that, he began to see the flash of a lake between the trees, then a sign for a little park. He turned and drove down the narrow road to a parking lot at the edge of the water, stopped the car and got out. There was a flatbed truck there and beside it a man unloading picnic tables. When Deshane got out of his car, the man nodded to him, but he didn't speak. He was tall with reddish hair and skin coarsened by the sun. He had long arms with tight ropy muscles and covered with blond hair, and he was unloading the truck alone. When the last of the tables was off, he got into the truck and drove away.

Deshane stood by the edge of the lake and looked out over the shining surface to the hills and islands beyond. Far out he thought he saw a boat and someone fishing. He looked over the surface of the lake, smooth and bright as mercury.

Norma stared out the front window of the store to where the street bridged the river, just above the waterfall. She studied The Fisherman. He'd been here every day for a week, on the concrete abutment by the river, with his folding chair, the tackle and bait. He sat there, a small thick figure with a round bald head, hunched on the chair, his rod in his hand, waiting, his fishing line vanishing in the slow deep water above the dam, thinking his thoughts or not thinking them. A stringer fastened to the leg of his chair hung down into the water beside the abutment, and it was impossible to tell if there were fish on the stringer, pickerel and perch, maybe even a big pike with its long jaw and malicious grin. Perhaps at the end of the day, he took them off and threw them back into the water that was the colour of clear coffee, and never took anything home, or maybe he took them home, all of them, every time, and gutted them and put them away in a freezer. If there were fish on the stringer. Did he catch any? She had never been sure. All day he sat there, and the sun brought out the freckles on his bald head, and his line was heavily enough weighted that it stayed still in the water. The current made a V shape around it, one branch of the V on each side of the line, and even when the cars went over the bridge, he didn't look up, just stared down into the brown clear water as if he could see the fish and as if his look were drawing them toward him. It was always when she wasn't watching that he arrived or left. When she looked he was there, or not there.

Right now, he was there, still, waiting. Norma was waiting too, for someone to come to her hook. The bait had just been dropped in the water. A sign hung in the front window of the store. COTTAGE FOR RENT. The young woman from Virginia, whose son took Norma out exploring in the middle of the night, had left and re-entered the Other Realm; people Norma knew nothing about, which was most of the world. Norma had an ad about to come out in the Kingston newspaper, but in the meantime, perhaps the sign in the window would draw someone. Most people who came here had their own places on the back lakes, or if they were travelling, they kept to the main roads, but she did see strangers about from time to time, and the cottage, which was on the other side of the main street, the first of a series of small places along the east bank of the river above the falls, had a broken-down dock that could be used for fishing or swimming or putting a boat in the water, so long as you did any of these things carefully. The dock ought to be repaired or replaced, but to build something that wouldn't be taken out by the ice in the spring would cost more money than Norma had. As things stood, the dock had posts on the bank and projected over the water, and she took over a hammer and nails from time to time and bashed on a new board here and there. That had been her system with the cottage, an occasional visit with a hammer and a lot of nails, and she was aware that the whole establishment lacked elegance. The pump wasn't very efficient and the storage tank wasn't very large, so you had to use water with discretion or the pump lost its prime and priming it could be a messy business, with water flying around. Damn cold when first done in the spring. A reminder that it was probably time to have the Shit Man come and pump out the holding tank. More money. She bought the cottage once when she was flush, thinking that property was always a good investment. Safe as houses. Never live by old sayings.

Last summer she did well enough. Even in September there was that sad and pretty little thing came out from the city looking for a place to recover from something mysterious, Bad Sex of one sort or another by the sounds of it, and she paid her rent and took invigorating swims in the river, seen once or twice running shivering through the cooling air back to the cottage. Miss Virginia, recently vanished, was charmed by the place at first, but she'd promised for a week and stayed only that.

Norma rocked in her favourite chair and looked through the sales book. Not a bad month now that she did the figures, if you kept in mind that there was never going to be a good month, and there were other things about life here, like waking in the night to hear the waterfall. She was, as they said, her own boss, though she was a discontented employee all the same, tempted to join a union and stick it to the management whenever possible. Demand a new contract. In a few months, she would get the old age pension, and that would help, her reward for hanging on all these years. Sell up and move to a little apartment in the city. Maybe.

She plugged in the electric kettle to make tea, and while it was heating went to the front window to check on The Fisherman. Nothing there. He was gone, and when she studied her watch, she discovered it was later than you think. Across the road on the shoulder just before the bend, there was a car parked, a big-old-fashioned-one, and beside it stood a man, also a big-old-fashioned-one, in a worn tweed jacket, tight in the shoulders, his hair combed straight back over his balding head, tossing his car keys in his hand, impatient and irritable, as if he'd been kept waiting for a hell of a time by some foolish woman. He was staring at her window. COTTAGE FOR RENT. Norma wondered if he could see her behind the glass, observing him, and wondered if seeing her would drive him away, and prudently slid out of sight, returned to the rocker. What will be will be. Maybe his wife was at the grocery store, and he was staring in the window while he waited for her to come back. She rocked some.

Carman opened the door of the shop and walked in. It was one big room, with a ceiling of pressed tin in ornate patterns painted over with white paint, walls with breaks in the plaster where old partitions had been torn down, and it was crowded with junk – china, magazines, books, furniture with more furniture piled on top. On the wall, an old fashioned photograph of a nude staring over her shoulder and beside it an ad for Royal Crown Cola. Some dresses and army uniforms hung on a rack, looking as if they might be full of fleas.

Near the back a woman sat in a rocking chair and stared at him. She didn't speak, only fixed her eyes on him as if waiting for him to tell her his business, and he thought he should get out before he started knocking things down and breaking them. You couldn't turn around without hitting a vase or a pile of plates.

There was a strange noise in the background, birds, and he looked around to see if she kept exotic creatures in cages. There was an old metal cage hanging on a metal stand near the back, but there was no bird in it. A click and the sound ended.

'That's the end of the tape,' the woman said. 'If you stand still you can hear the waterfall.' She was heavy, and she sank down into the chair as if she had no intention of getting up. She was wearing a black suit jacket over a black turtleneck sweater, and the sweater emphasized her jowls.

'I know,' she said, as if she'd read his mind, 'I'm a fat old woman and that's about all. You looking for something in particular or driven by random curiosity?'

She was still staring at him.

'I saw the sign,' he said.

'You want to rent the cottage?'

For the first time, she showed a little interest and began to get out of the chair. Straightened up with a tiny groan.

'It's on the river,' she said. 'The other side of the road.'

'I just stopped to look around,' he said.

'The best decisions are made in obedience to a sudden impulse.'

Carman didn't answer. He still felt as if there might be bugs crawling out of things and touching him. The woman was walking down the shop toward him, studying him as if trying to decide whether to reach out and touch him, perhaps to push him out the door.

'Shall we go and have a look?' she said.

'I didn't plan to rent it.'

'You just thought you'd come in and bother me for nothing.'

'The store's open, isn't it?'

'It's business hours,' she said.

She was close to him now, and he was aware of her big stomach, bisected by the line of the belt on her black slacks. Audrey had always kept herself thin.

'Are you going to look at the cottage?'

'Yes.'

She pointed to the front door, and once they were outside, she turned the sign from Open to Closed and locked the door.

'The Fisherman's gone,' she said. 'First he's there, and then he's not.'

Carman didn't answer. It didn't seem to have anything to do with him. They crossed the road, went along a hundred feet to a sideroad and turned left over the gravel where the unpaved road joined the pavement, then down a slope. The sideroad was shaded by a row of old maples. Down by the river, flat and dark and smooth with little ripples of current, there were a couple of willows growing. The cottage sat above the ground on concrete blocks and heavy pieces of squared timber, and underneath it, chained to one of the concrete blocks, was an old rowboat painted green. Once, when he and Audrey were first married, they rented a cottage for a couple of weeks with a boat like that. They fell out of it one night while they were trying to make love on one of the wooden seats.

The woman was going up the stairs to the back door.

'Watch your step,' she said.

There were broken boards on the steps and on the porch.

'You'd want to get that fixed,' he said.

'Would I?'

'You could fall through.'

'One of these days.'

She led him inside the cottage. It was furnished, more or less, and it looked clean. From the back door where they'd come in, you could look through the kitchen past the small living room and out a wide front window to see the willows and the river, the old dock.

'How much are you asking?' he said.

'How long are you saying?'

'Depends how much you're asking.'

'Depends how long you're staying.'

She was staring at him again. He didn't like it.

'Why are you staring at me?'

'Am I?'

'Yes.'

'Tough tittie,' she said.

'All right,' he said. 'Let's forget the whole thing.'

'You're a bad-tempered man.'

Carman was beginning to feel a pressure in his chest and wondered if he should take a pill. He wasn't going to do it in front of this woman. He started for the door.

'You thinking about a week?' she said. 'Two weeks?'

'I'm not planning on anything.'

'Take it for the rest of the summer, I'll give you a good price.'

He stopped and looked back at her. Over her shoulder, he saw the three chairs and a small table that were the furniture in the living room, and beyond that the window, the grass, the river flowing darkly past the grey dock. A bird flew low over the water, blue and quick, a kingfisher, sunlight on its wings.

'All right,' he said. 'I'll take it.'

'For how long?'

'The summer if the price is right.'

She named a price, until Labour Day. Cheaper than the motel, and she offered to throw in sheets and towels.

'But you wash them yourself,' she said. 'I'm nobody's washerwoman.'

She was staring at him again.

'You got a laundromat here?'

'Nope. Down the road another ten miles.'

It was hard to get used to the fact that these things mattered now, where you washed your clothes, bought groceries. Audrey had sheltered him from all that. The fat woman stared. Abruptly she held out her hand.

'Norma,' she said.

He didn't want to shake her hand, but he had no choice. It was warm in his, and her grip was firm.

'Carman Deshane,' he said.

'You moving in right away?'

'I'll stay the night,' he said, 'then I have to go and pick up some stuff. I'll give you a cheque for a month.'

'Come back to the store, and I'll get you the sheets and towels.'

He'd started the day miles from here, with no thought that

anything like this would happen. Now he'd rented a cottage from a woman he didn't like. When they got back to the store, he wrote a cheque. The woman had mumbled something and left him standing while she disappeared through a doorway and thumped up the stairs. He waited a long time. She was taking forever, and he stood helpless and irritable, looking over all the rubbish she was selling and wondering who would put out money for any of it. Beside the front door were two electric stoves with stains on the enamel, and above them on the wall hung some sort of banner from an Orange Lodge. An oak filing cabinet with little drawers, the kind you'd find in an old library. The Queen smiled down three times from the wall above. Across from her, Royal Crown Cola and the photograph of the nude, her hair long and wavy, her head back and looking over her shoulder and into the air, her body shapely but not the current fashion, the proportions too big and classic. The woman appeared at the bottom of the stairs and noticed him staring at the photograph.

'Good-looking girl,' she said. 'We all were, once upon a time.'

She had a heavy-footed walk, and she came toward him as if she might barge past and knock him down, but stopped and put the piles of towels and bedding in his arms. He thanked her and turned to leave.

'Wait a minute,' she said, and pushed between two tables and took down the photograph of the nude. 'I'll throw this in as part of the deal. Long-term loan, to cheer the place up a little.'

'I don't want that goddam thing,' he said.

'Why not?'

'I just don't want it.' He wouldn't have her making fun of him.

'A pretty girl,' she said. 'Not quite art, but nice all the same. You imagine some photographer in 1952 admiring that pretty body and getting her to come to his studio and show herself. Daring thing in those days. When I look at that I wonder where she is now, getting older, husband with Alzheimer's, thinking about how long it will all go on. You wonder if she still has that picture of herself, her big perfect body.'

'I've got no use for the goddam thing.'

She was staring at him again, as if she knew something but wouldn't say it.

'I guess you're not interested,' she said.

He didn't answer, just turned and walked out. He couldn't help it, and he blamed her for making him do that. He wanted the cottage, but he wanted her to leave him alone. Crazy old bitch. He called her that and worse all the way along the road and down to the cottage, feeling like a fool with the pile of bedding in his arms. After he made the bed, he went to the trunk of the car and got out his box of papers and photographs, never unpacked at the motel, and he put the picture of Audrey on the table by the front window.

The next day, Carman drove to Toronto through the busy summer traffic of Highway 401, went to the motel and packed up his possessions. He'd been there less than a week, and Doug refunded him part of what he'd paid. Carman hadn't expected anything, but the man was quick to make the offer, an odd look on his handsome ruined face as if he was frightened, a look Carman had often seen when he was a cop, but he couldn't understand why he was seeing it now. Still, he took the money.

When he got everything into the car, he was exhausted, so he lay down on the bed and slept for an hour, then decided to explore the bit of bush behind the motel before getting back on the road. All along the creekbed, there was an earth wall that had been built to hold back the water when the stream flooded in the spring. The motel had been built on the floodplain, and it wouldn't take much to inundate it. The dike was covered with grass and the sides were steep, but here and there a path led up to the top and down the other side. Then there was a path that led along the creek, a place for people to get a bit of air or walk their dogs. There wasn't a lot of water in the creek now, but here and there you saw deep holes.

The bush was mostly scrub. Manitoba maples, sometimes a big bent willow hanging over the water, bushes that he couldn't identify growing in clumps. Where the banks narrowed, you could hear the babble of water. He stood there by one of these riffles and listened, aware that behind the chattering of the water, he could still hear the cars on the highway. That steady hum, like a hive of bees.

The water was shallow here, the bottom sandy with an occasional round rock. Then, as he watched, a huge fish appeared, like some water monster, so big that it had to force its way through the shallows, its back out of water, the tail flapping wildly to drive it forward over the sand, and it was gone into the deeper pool on the other side.

He couldn't believe what he'd seen, a fish that size in this little creek. The creek emptied into Lake Ontario not many miles away, and the fish must have made its way up from the lake, a huge carp, or one of the salmon that they'd planted since the lampreys were under control and the lake a little less polluted. Whatever it was, he decided to walk upstream and see if it came into sight again in the next shallows. It must mean something, that great fish. He followed the path, but ahead of him, the path turned away from the stream and went round a section of thick undergrowth beneath two willows. He was sweating as he pushed his way through the bushes, but he wanted to stay close to the bank of the stream, watching for the thick dark form of the fish. A branch had fallen into the water here, and other pieces of wood floating down had caught on it, creating a kind of dam and the water rippled noisily over it.

As he stared down into the water looking for his sea monster, he saw something waving in the water like a weed, like a small white human hand. Then it was gone. He looked at the light in the riffles of water, the slick surface and brown depths, a Styrofoam cup on the sand of the low bank on the other side. The air was thin and resonant, and he had the crazy feeling that a murder had taken place somewhere in this bit of abandoned land. The body thrown into the creek. Then it was as if he might be the murderer but had forgotten it all, and they were coming for him. He had to get out of here. Always, over the sound of the stream, he could hear the cars and trucks on the highway. He could feel the hard beating of his heart, and all of his life was coming toward him, to find him here. Or was it his death? He looked back toward the water, searching for the white waving hand, but he saw only a tangle of branches, current pulling weeds. He made his way back along the stream to the motel where he washed up, splashed cold water on his face, took his pills. It was time to go. He'd find somewhere for lunch and then get away from the city and drive back to the cottage he'd rented.

Late that night, Carman stood by the other river, the one that ran past the cottage and listened to night noises, frogs crying out whatever it was frogs cried out, a sound of water running among reeds, wind, the waterfall. Around all these sounds there was something bigger, a silence around the noise in the way that around the glittering stars there was darkness. Something clean and terrible. Earlier in the evening he'd sat by the back window with the pages he'd once written about his first days on the corvette, and read over the words. What he'd written didn't really tell what it had been like, the metallic edge to all the sounds, the way the whole boat vibrated with the power of the engine that drove it through the water. How close and narrow every passage was, the low doorways. The smell of the sea air and the bitter smoke from the funnels. He hadn't said those things, but when he read the bare narrative, he could remember them, and he didn't need to write them down. The first officer named McCann, ill-humoured and with an exceptionally foul mouth even among young and rough-spoken sailors. There was the satisfaction of having your whole world close at hand, and the knowledge that out there in the fog there were other ships, and perhaps a storm looking for you.

That was what he recalled, or thought he did. It was a long time ago now, and there was a lot that you didn't remember, as if, for days on end, you hadn't lived at all. It was gone. Carman brushed away a mosquito, turned from the river and walked through the darkness back toward the house, and as he did, he looked toward the next-door cottage and saw through the window the young woman who lived there, as she stood in the lighted kitchen, washing dishes. She had two small girls; he'd seen them in the yard when he got back. She had come over to say hello when she saw him unpacking the car. Amy. After she had introduced herself, she stood smiling at him as if waiting for him to tell her his story or to ask for hers. Carman thought that she wanted to tell him more than he cared to know. She was tall, slim, dressed in shorts, her legs pale and thin, but she had large breasts that seemed flagrant and misplaced on her slender body. There was no sign of a man at the cottage. The place was built on a mortared block foundation and had aluminum windows, as if they lived there all year. Carman watched her through his wide window and wondered whether he would get to know her. There was something uneasy, discontented, about her face, the way she moved.

Norma unplugged the whistling kettle and poured boiling water into the filter over the three tablespoons of coffee. It was a good smell, and she turned the stove to simmer and went to the table to eat her shredded wheat. Which was good for her as the coffee wasn't. There were more and more things that weren't good for you, and odd things that were. From time to time, she liked to get dried fruit and nuts from a health food store in the city, and while she was there, she would stare in astonishment at the bottles of magic pills. If she went to the right kind of practitioner, she would be told to choke down some of these things. Pills made from roots and weeds and dirt. Eat dirt and you won't hurt. Unfortunately, she didn't believe it. There was a new pain in the back of her head this morning, also in her legs. The headbone's connected. Days you'd wish it disconnected.

One cup of coffee done, she took the second to the bedroom and began to get herself dressed. There was a mirror on the door of the closet and mostly she avoided it. Her shape grew more and more that of an egg. An egg with a leg and another leg. She had to sit down to pull on her pants and socks, and she worked away at it all, panting now and then, and soon enough she was kitted up for the day, all in green like one of Robin Hood's merry men. Somewhere in the closet was an old green hat with a feather that would complete the effect, and she poked through dead things until she found it and set it on her head. Raffish. That was a kind word for how she must look, but it did her heart good to be absurd. In celebration, she would do dishes and make the bed.

It was an hour or so later, as she was going down the stairs to open the shop, that she remembered once again that her cottage was rented for the rest of the summer. Hooray for the bucks. Ill-tempered son of a bitch, though, with a murderous look in his eyes. Maybe hiding out from the law and she would learn that he had a string of bloody killings to his credit. Still, he paid. Unless the cheque bounced. Yesterday he'd gone off to get his possessions: say, guns, knives, instruments of torture. What did a thumbscrew look like?

Norma had brought the pot of coffee downstairs with her, and she put it on the hotplate at the back of the shop and popped a tape into the player and got something nebulous and soothing. Not as good as the birds. The sun was shining in the back window and making a pattern on the set of kitchen chairs, shapes of light falling on the red paint. Beautiful, you said, and then wondered how a thing got to be beautiful. Norma checked her watch and decided it was too early to make the phone calls on her list, which were anyway people wanting to sell and what she needed was people wanting to buy. Upstairs she had some very early copies of the *Saturday Evening Post*, and there was a dealer in Toronto who might take them if she offered to pack them up and put them in the mail. She went to the front door, unfastened the lock and turned the sign round. Now she was open for business. She tried to see whether her tenant had left the cottage, but the driveway was hidden behind a clump of elders. While it was morning and her joints still loose from a hot bath, she should bring up some of the books from the basement, price them and get them on shelves. It was so much easier to do nothing. Shut off the tape, which was so soothing it made her furious, and turned on the radio. Talk or music: she chose music and found CBC Stereo was playing something lively and pleasant. She couldn't tell one composer from another, but she knew what she didn't like. Heavy stuff, that's what she didn't like.

On the way down the back stairs, she caught the long pheasant feather of her hat on the edge of the trap door, and the hat flipped off, but when she got to the bottom of the stairs, she put it firmly back on, collected a cardboard box of books and laboured up the stairs with them, a lot of puffing but she got there, and when she did rewarded herself with a cup of coffee and a little sit in the rocking chair. It creaked when she sat down, a tribute to her fatness, and that made her talk back a little, but then she sipped coffee and rocked contentedly, and closed her eyes, and thinking she might fall asleep, she set the coffee aside and let the hypnagogic images that were lurking at the edges of her eyes come out to play.

The bell on the door woke her, but by the time she had her eyes open, the man was standing close to her, watching. A thin beard and a greasy cap pulled down on his forehead, pants tucked into rubber boots. His thin chest dropped in a long curve to the sag of a pot belly, and he had long arms that hung loosely at his sides, fingernails that looked like the claws of an animal. Out of the back country to the north.

'Well?' she said.

There was a honking noise, and it took her a second to realize that it was his speech. He had a cleft palate. These things could be repaired now, but where he lived, the news hadn't arrived. Norma got her wits together, get herself up from the chair, but the man didn't move to give her space, just stayed where he was. She wanted to push him away.

'I was asleep,' she said. 'You startled me.' She hoped he'd repeat himself without being asked. He did, and it became clear that he wanted to show her something on his truck, and when she had agreed to that, he turned and walked to the door, his rubber boots scuffing against the floor as he moved. He threw open the door when he reached it, and she caught it on the way back and let herself through to where his small truck was parked, right in front of the store. He pointed to the back and honked. Norma went to look.

Ten glass eyes looked at her. Sunlight on fur. Five of them in life-like postures that exaggerated their deadness. A raccoon, a weasel, a mink, a squirrel and a wolf, stuffed and mounted. Creative taxidermy: the squirrel was climbing a branch, the raccoon stood by the stump of a small tree, the others were posed on varnished pine. They were old, and the fur had a dusty look, but there was no obvious damage. Though she was used to dealing with the world's abandoned things, the sight of these animals gave Norma a chill, and she wondered where the man had found them. Maybe he'd stuffed them himself in earlier years, had read an ad in a magazine and sent away for the course in do-it-yourself taxidermy then gone about the woods killing things.

'How much do you want?'

'Twenty.' Or that's what it sounded like.

'For the lot?'

He looked as if that wasn't what he had in mind, but then he nodded. Norma reached into her pocket where she kept a small stash of bills and took out two tens and handed them over. He put them in his shirt pocket and reached into the truck to begin unloading. Took the wolf first thing. Norma had just picked up the squirrel on its branch when she was aware of car doors opening and saw, a few steps in front of the truck, a man coming toward her, a man with a familiar face. Oh. Oh God. It was her son, Arthur, and there was an unknown young woman with him.

'Don't just stand about,' she said. 'Pick up a creature and come in.'

The man in the rubber boots had walked to the back of the store and set the wolf on top of a round oak dining table. Norma set the squirrel beside it and turned to go back. The narrow aisle between the pieces of furniture was crowded by the man with the cleft palate, Arthur holding the raccoon and its stump and his girl carrying the mink and the weasel. She was maybe thirty, and she was smiling. There was a little dance, and the two of them came toward her, as the rubber boots of her other visitor scuffed their way to the door. Norma took the raccoon from Arthur and put it beside the other two animals. She'd have to get a hairbrush to get some of the dust out of the fur of these new arrivals. As she stood there in her Robin Hood costume – Lincoln green, wasn't that what they wore, those cute thieves? – she was aware that Arthur and his new squeeze – must be that – were trying not to stare at her hat with its long draggled feather reaching out toward them. She could have taken it off, but wouldn't.

'Mother,' Arthur said, 'this is my friend Julie.'

Norma took the mink from the woman and put it on her desk among the disorderly pile of receipts and phone numbers and unpaid bills. The girl wasn't pretty, though some might have called her handsome, square bony sort of body, short hair, slightly crooked face with sharp hazel eyes. Norma offered a hand, which was taken and crushed. She must be one of those weightlifters.

'What happened to your wife?' she said to Arthur.

'I told you we'd split up, last year.'

'You did no such thing.'

'I did.'

'Never heard a word of it.'

'I remember perfectly well.'

'You're making it all up.'

'I phoned you one night.' He was starting to get angry. She always made him angry, and she sometimes enjoyed it. 'When I phoned you were …'. He stopped.

'Drunk may be the word you're looking for.'

Julie was looking around the place.

'Not on the booze any more,' Norma said to her. 'For a while I was treating my aches and pains with large doses of vodka and forgetting things. After a bit I decided I was feeling more worse than better.'

'Have you tried acupuncture?' Julie said eagerly.

'No. Foolish business.'

Looked offended. Gave a glance at the hat.

'How old are you?' Norma said. Compounding the offence and enjoying it.

'Twenty-nine.'

'Arthur must be getting on for forty by now, aren't you, Arthur?'

'You must know how old I am.'

'It's all a blur, those years before Steven took flight with his bimbo. I was thinking about Steven the other day. Is he still with that girl?'

It was a long time ago, but not long enough.

'No, he's not.'

'I hope she left him for some young stud.'

'I'm not sure.'

'Yes you are, but you're being loyal.'

She turned to Julie who was standing with her head drawn in a little, like a boxer ready to feint and counterpunch.

'Are you and Arthur planning to stay together or is he just dipping his wick?'

The young woman burst out laughing.

'I've never heard that expression before,' she said. 'It's very colourful.'

'I'm full of colourful expressions,' Norma said. 'I'm sure that's why Arthur brought you to see me.'

'We came because I insisted.'

'Why would you do that?'

'I wanted to meet you.'

'Why? Because he said I was a terrible old bitch, and you thought it was a challenge.'

'Of course not.'

'Now that I think of it,' Norma said, 'I do remember getting a call. It was from Margaret. She said you'd found a bimbo too.'

Margaret was the abandoned wife. Norma had been in her cups when the woman called, dutiful or weepy, it was all pretty vague, but if she remembered right, she hadn't been able to do much but suggest that Margaret hire someone to cut the balls off her erring son. Nobody had said anything in response to her last sally, so she went right on.

'So he left Margaret for your sweet ways?' she said to the young woman.

'No, we met just last month at a party.'

'What is it you see in him?'

'You're his mother, you must know.'

Norma looked at her son, and for a moment she did, and then she didn't.

'Somebody go lock the front door, and we'll go upstairs and I'll make some fresh coffee.'

No, they weren't going to do that, it appeared, were on their way to Toronto in a rush and had only dropped in for a quick look at the old monster. Norma said a few more objectionable things and stuck out her tongue at them as they left. Arthur was a stick, and not even this bright young thing would make him anything more than that. All her fault, no doubt; she'd been a respectable person while he was little and had liked his nice-little-boy manners. Ugh. Not long after they drove away, Amy Martyrdom from the cottage down the way came in to talk, her big breasts hanging disconsolately inside a white T-shirt, and while her two little girls checked out the stuffed animals and then wandered around breaking things, she admired Norma's foolish hat, drank stale coffee and chattered about masturbation and whether the lesbian option was right for her. Norma liked Amy Martyrdom, though she couldn't have said why, and she listened patiently to all this, thinking again what a strange world it was that this not unattractive young woman was dying of loneliness and couldn't manage to get a leg thrown over her from time to time. Once upon a time, couples stayed together and kept off the beast that way.

Carman had slept well, and this morning he had walked along the short main street past the deserted hotel to the side road that led down to the river below the falls; now he stood on the concrete wall above the thickly twined, rushing water of the millrace, surrounded by the noise, and looked upward to the buildings at the top of the ravine. Trees cut him off from the sky, and light was reflected off water and granite and hanging green weed. As he looked up from his vantage point at the edge of the falling water, he could see the back of the buildings above. Something fateful and dangerous about standing here, as if the houses might suddenly tumble down the hill toward him. He turned and looked downriver from his green cave of leaves, into a huge sunlit space, sky and fields. Below the falls, where the river grew wider, was a field of tangled grasses and weeds, wild barley, daisies, buttercups, the red branches and pale leaves of flowering dogwood, and over the fields, the wild canaries rose and dipped in their characteristic flight, never far above the safety of the earth, yellow as the buttercups, black as coal.

He looked back up the stream toward the waterfall and thought he saw something moving at the edge of the water, a bird or animal, but it was gone again. The sound went on, unchanging, and the water ran close to him, and he took deep breaths of the wet air. It was all new to him; he'd never been in this place before. The world was full of things you've never seen. Once Audrey got him a subscription to *National Geographic* for Christmas, and now and then on a weekend, he'd sit down with the magazine and look at the pictures of other countries, read about them, but at the end of the year, he told her not to renew the subscription. He didn't want to spend his life reading about places he'd never get to. He knew there were men who went on for years living that way. It took all kinds. Being a cop you saw that. A few years back, Carman took things for granted, but now, retired, knowing that he was in bad shape, he looked back, and everything in his life was unlikely and strange. Would Audrey have understood that if he'd tried to tell her? Maybe. He had too much time on his hands now, too much time to think. Carol was right; he should have a hobby, but it was too late, and he didn't know what a hobby might be for a man like him. Not working with his hands: he could change a washer if necessary, put weatherstripping on a door, but those were things you did in order to have them done, not for their own sake. He looked back up at the waterfall. For centuries, perhaps millennia, there had been a waterfall here where the slow river, draining the land above, had made a path that led it over a granite cliff and then rapidly among rocks for the next hundred yards until once again it began to flow tranquilly through flat land and wide patches of marsh. The years told their story over and over, an old sleepy song of long winters, the earth buried in heavy drifts of snow, and then in spring the rapid melting, rivers high and dangerous, the waterfall heavy, brown with mud, loud in the cool nights, then in the long dry summer, the water coming with less urgent power, and clear as it made its way between the boulders at the foot of the little cataract.

Settlers arrived, and on every river someone built a mill, as they had just where he stood, where the situation was perfect, a good drop, a kind of plateau halfway down the hill for the building, only a small dam needed to direct the water into the millrace. Maybe the first mill burned down, as mills so often did, and was rebuilt. A village grew around it. Now the mill was gone, derelict for a long time, and finally torn down, only the foundations left, the millrace. The hotel, built for travellers in the good days, was a ruin.

He turned away from the river and started along the path that would lead him back up to the street, thinking about his father, how he would set out in the dark on cold winter mornings to go to work in the Halifax shipyards, and Carman would say to himself that he wasn't going to end up like that, rising obediently every day and doing what he was told. What he'd done wasn't much different after all, a few years in the navy, then he went to Toronto and pounded a beat and met Audrey and started to work in plain clothes and now it was over. You dropped in your ticket and rode the streetcar to the end of the line, or maybe you took a transfer, another one, but the cars only ran so far.

Carman walked up the narrow road to the main street very slowly, and when he got there he wasn't too short of breath. There was an old man on a chair fishing from the concrete abutment at the edge of the bridge, and as Carman walked down the side road toward the cottage, the two little girls from the cottage next door were splashing around in the water at the edge of the river, naked in the sunlight. Their mother sat on a folding chair nearby.

Norma was grooming her wolf when the tenant arrived. She had bought a cheap hairbrush from the grocery store and she was brushing the hair of her new stuffed wolf, getting a lot of dust and dirt out of him. The creature was starting to look quite handsome, glass eyes wiped with spit and Kleenex and now very bright. She looked toward her tenant, the putative murderer, who was coming toward her. She could tell he was mad from the way he opened the door.

'What's wrong now?' she said.

'The water,' he said.

'You ran it too long. Lost the prime on the pump.'

'All I did was take a shower.'

'You shouldn't do that.'

'What am I supposed to do?'

'You've got a whole river at your back door.'

'I don't know what kind of an outfit it is if you can't even use the shower.'

'You can if you don't stay in too long. It wasn't made for you to stand around in hot water playing with yourself.'

His eyes went hard. Norma was afraid of him at that moment, but there didn't appear to be anything to do but wait. He looked away, took a deep breath, gathered himself together.

'Do you get it fixed?' he said. 'Or do I just do without water.'

'I'll show you how to prime it,' she said. 'Then next time you can fix it for yourself.'

At the back of the store, she kept a little canvas bag of tools. She went and got it and met him at the front door. Her back and legs were stiff today, and she had to work hard to keep herself chugging along at a normal rate and looking like a real human being. The man didn't speak.

'You're retired,' she said.

'Mmm.'

'What did you do when you were still alive?'

'Cop.'

They were going down the slope of the gravel road and Norma was afraid she might fall.

'Are they all as bad-tempered as you?'

'No.'

Norma didn't say anything more, partly because she was a little out of breath from the walk, which had gone too fast for her.

When they got up to the side of the cottage, she led the way to the corner where the plastic pipe came in from the river.

'Which one of us is going underneath?' she said.

'You have to crawl underneath?'

'That's the pump in there.' She pointed to where the small blue pump sat bolted to a board that was wired to a couple of concrete blocks. It was a jerry-built arrangement, but it worked.

'We need some water,' she said and set off down to the river with an old pot that was left hanging on a block of wood that held up the corner of the cottage. The edge was weedy but the dock was high out of the water, and she wasn't sure which was the more dangerous to her in her crippled state. When she got close, she saw a big stone among the reeds, and she managed to get a foot on that without falling in and got the pan half full of water. Getting her foot back off the stone was harder than it appeared, and a toe was dampened a little. The man stood by the side of the building waiting for her. A cop. Imagine that. At a distance, his face was all dark lines, eyebrows, thinning hair, mouth, a hard jaw. Mr Law and Order. She crossed the grass to where he waited.

'I'll go underneath,' he said, 'if you tell me what to do.'

She handed him a set of vise-grips, then she took a metal cup out of her bag and gave him that and the pot.

'There's a metal plug on the top that screws in and out,' she said. 'You take that out and fill the chamber underneath with water. Then I'll turn it on from the reset button over there and we hope for the best.'

He put the vise-grips in his pocket and crawled on his hands and knees the few feet to the pump, pushing the pot of water along beside him.

'Is this it?' he said, pointing to the hexagonal nut on the top.

'That's it.'

He unscrewed the nut and began pouring cups of water into the chamber.

'How much?' he said.

'Till it looks full.'

He poured in some more water, then looked back toward her.

Norma went to the switch under the edge of the cottage, beside the nail where she hung the pot. She turned on the pump which whirred a little, bubbled, and then shot up a geyser of water. What didn't catch him on the way up splashed back down on him from the floorboards.

'Jesus Christ!'

He looked darker, sodden, more murderous, and Norma felt a certain perverse pleasure in his discomfiture. He wouldn't be taking any more long showers. But she knew better than to laugh out loud.

'Keep pouring in water.'

He filled the cup and poured it into the small hole. The pump was bubbling out air.

'Keep pouring in a little at a time as the air bubbles out. When you hear it starting to suck water put the nut back in.'

The man crouched under the building and Norma sat on the grass to watch him. In a minute or so, she could hear the water coming up.

'There,' she said.

The man crawled out, wiped his face with a handkerchief then stood, brushed off his trousers, dumped the water back out of the pot and hung it in its place. He handed the vise-grips to her.

'Thank you,' he said.

Well, she thought, at least he isn't a whiner.

'If you spelt vise-grips with a c, it would make a new name for the police,' she said. 'The Vice-grips.'

He looked at her as if she were a crazy woman. Maybe she was.

'Why don't you have the pump out here where you could get at it?'

'I don't know. It was under there when I bought the cottage, and I've just never moved it.'

'I'll see you later,' he said, and without another word went to the back porch of the cottage and up the broken stairs. As Norma watched him go in, she reflected that she really should get this and that repaired. This and that and the other. Someday. She started back up the road. Her dead animals were waiting for her.

The great blue heron he'd been watching as it stood in the shallow water by the dock flew away and night fell on the river. As the days passed, all these things grew familiar. Now it was dark, he could go to bed, or read a book, or turn on the little television set he'd bought and see what he could pick up with the built-in aerial, or he could just sit here in a comfortable chair beside the window looking from darkness into darkness as minutes went by, as the river flowed past, a light down by the bridge reflected on the surface. If you looked upriver, you knew that the water was there in the night but you couldn't see it. Off through the trees, light in a window, small and far off. Someone else's life.

A pale ghost crossing the grass toward the river. The long white body of his neighbour gone skinny-dipping after the children were asleep. Her pale dim shape was almost invisible now as she walked into the water, only a hint of something in the darkness, then she dived in and he could see nothing. He picked up the glass of rye and sipped from it, waited for her to come out. A peeping Tom now. But he hadn't sought her out. Or so he might say, though he had known as he sat here that she would appear. You knew things without knowing how. Rolly joked about that, Carman's magic powers. Carman the Mentalist, he called him. It was true that if they walked into a place where someone on the staff was stealing, Carman would know pretty quickly who it was, whether or not he could prove it. Nothing magic about it, just had to pay attention. He could smell it, he used to say. You knew more than you knew. He had walked by that stream behind the motel, and he'd known that once, however long ago, a death had happened there. Just as he'd known that tonight his young neighbour would go naked across the yard to swim in the river. In a certain kind of book, she would come to his door instead of returning to her own house, and he would welcome her in and take her to bed. Things that happened in books. He took another sip of whisky and watched the river. Something moved. She was climbing out of the water. As she came closer, he could almost make out the shape of her big breasts against the long slender body, and he drew back from the window into his chair, lest she see him there observing.

Just before she disappeared from his view, she looked toward him. Yet he swore that she couldn't see him here in the dark. She imagined him here, watching, was pleased to be seen, looked toward him so he would know.

She was gone, but he sat perfectly still, waiting for the knock on the door. Time was passing again, in rapid heartbeats now. He was a sick old man and she would have no interest, and yet when she came across to introduce herself, there was a hunger in her eyes, she flirted a little, a hint of craziness, or maybe just being too lonely. Carman picked up the glass of rye and tasted it in his mouth and down his throat and thought about what it would be like to have a woman in his bed. A stranger. They said human contact helped to keep you alive. Or any kind of contact. For a while Carol had tried to convince him he should get a dog or a cat. She had a couple of kittens when she was little, and watching them, Carman had concluded that cats were a lot like some of the criminals he pursued, all nerve and driven to destroy, the big kitten eyes staring out of the narrow head as it raced about looking for something to kill.

He heard the knock almost without knowing it. What he had imagined. Had she waited out there all this time? He turned on a light as he went to the door, his heart beating fast. Opened the door and found Norma standing there, her head sunk into her shoulders, eyes fixed on him with that hard stare.

'Keys to unlock the boat,' she said, and reached out. 'Forgot them before.'

He took the keys, and she turned away and started down the steps.

'Watch your step,' he said.

'I know,' she said. 'The goddam porch needs fixing. I'll get to it.'

She was vanishing into the darkness.

'One of these days I'll do it,' he shouted after her. 'You can pay for the wood.'

'Don't bother your little head about it,' she said.

Carman closed the door behind her and stood for a minute

with the keys in his hand. The boat. Not sure he'd ever bother to take it out. He tossed the keys on the kitchen table. Well, the knock at the door had come, hadn't it? Now he'd go and take a pill and get into bed to finish that paperback about the destruction of the world by new kinds of germs.

Norma was trying to think about things, to be orderly and systematic and reach a conclusion. She'd gone through all this before, it was one of her techniques on nights when she couldn't sleep. Trying to figure out what thinking was and do it. It was better than TV. She lay in her bed, aching in this part and that, and wondered if she could have a few smart thoughts about pain. A stimulation of the nerves that warned you of damage being done, or damage that had been done. It was possible that the night was full of people who were not experiencing pain, though there might be those whose pain was worse, whose pain was excruciating. Excruciating: whatever that meant. If she didn't fall asleep soon, maybe she'd get up and look up excruciating in the Shorter Oxford. From (fire up the high school Latin) *crux*, cross? Like the pain of being on a cross? Now it was getting all theological. Was God responsible for pain and why would God invent such a thing?

This wasn't thinking, not what she had in mind at all. Pain exists. Next step in the syllogism was what? One, two, ergo three. *Quod erat demonstrandum.* Always liked the arrogant certainty of that old tag, not that she'd ever thought anything was proved by formal logic. What was proved was that if you dropped a man out a window, he would hit the ground. Proved enough, though there was always the possible day when the sun didn't rise and bodies floated upward into the air. Wasn't there? And was this thinking? Ruminating, which, as she remembered was what a cow did with its food. Another word to look up, but by the time she gave up on sleep, she would have forgotten all these linguistic duties.

Excruciating. Crucifixion had got all tangled up with Christ and martyrs, but it was a common punishment, the Romans were at it all the time, malefactors (always liked that word) artistically draped over their wooden frames on every hilltop. Make them suffer. How did the pain of crucifixion compare with what her body went through on a bad day? Well, the exacerbation of the nerves didn't kill her, though on the very worst days, she wished it would. All right, Norma, enough of that. That's not thinking, it's whining. Change the subject. To what? The Vice-grip in her cottage. She liked her joke even though he hadn't the wit to appreciate it. She could design a whole new TV series. The Vice-grips. She had taken a certain delight is seeing him crawling sodden out from under the cabin, trying to resurrect his dignity. Sad critters, men, so delicate and touchy, of limited use for fetching and carrying and screwing. As she walked along the dark road to the cottage a few nights ago, going to give him the boat keys, she'd caught a glimpse of Amy Martyrdom strolling naked across the lawn after a skinnydip in the river. The lights were off in Carman The Vice-grip's cottage when she arrived; he must have been watching Amy running around in the buff. Now there was a phrase that needed looking up. One of those antiquated things she'd picked up from her mother. That impossible woman that she grew more and more to resemble.

She should keep a pad and pencil by her bed to make notes of all the things she wanted to look up. One of the advantages of her business was that she got good books for a song, and over the years she had made herself a very satisfying reference library. She'd always hoped to get the complete Oxford in all its many volumes, but never had. The Book-of-the-Month Club version with the magnifying glass had turned up, but she couldn't read it even with the big lens. Then there was the dictionary of classical Greek that she'd been unable to resist even though she didn't know the Greek alphabet. Elegant mysterious shapes, sinuous and oriental. That was a project, she'd once thought, for her old age, but now she was well on her way to old age with no sign of Greek being learned today or tomorrow. Or even the day after tomorrow. In the long cold winter nights perhaps.

She turned and felt a new stab of crucifixion. They said you felt all this in your brain, but it sure seemed like the hips and legs to her. It's all in your head, my dear. Also in her head was a growing desire for a cup of cocoa. She rolled over, got an arm under her and pushed herself up to a sitting position, then with another push, got standing and went for her dressing gown. Back in the kitchen, she opened the inside door. A mosquito hung on the screen and beyond was the sound of the waterfall. Sometimes at night like this, she heard voices singing, a woman and a man on the balcony of the old hotel lining out Victorian ballads, pretty tunes in lovely harmony, but she could never quite get the words. Or it was angels who sang without words, only strange sounds, or the words that might be formed by those sinuous Greek letters in the old lexicon? Yes, everyone knew that angels sang in Greek. *Kyrie, kyrie, kyrie.* The earth in robes of melody, the words from the oldest of old times. The angels of night and summer sang, incomprehensible and sweet. She would drink her cup of cocoa and listen to their mystic adorations.

The days went by. He watched the flowing river, the birds. They were good days, though he knew his heart was failing, the end waiting close by. Now once again the light was going, and Carman was about ready for bed. He pulled open the drawer where he kept his clothes to find pyjamas. He'd thrown everything in one drawer when he arrived, and now it was time enough to sort things. Not that he had many clothes, but he took out some polo shirts and opened the bottom drawer to put them in. From the bottom of the empty drawer, a photograph of his own face looked up at him. What kind of joke was this? He took out the old newspaper and threw it on the bed, put away the shirts and then picked it up again. The *Toronto Star*, six years ago. Detectives Deshane and Menard arresting a suspect in the murder of little Melanie Ovett, his own face hard and blank as the camera clicked away and he and Rolly, one holding each arm, took the creep into the station. They'd been the ones to find the little girl too, her body stuffed behind a ventilation shaft in the basement of the apartment building. Carman remembered when he found her, he started to cry – he couldn't help it, but he got hold of himself, Rolly never saw it – and that was when he began to think about retiring. You saw bad things and heard about worse, but when he saw that pile of rubbish that was a kid, could have been his daughter once, he wanted to find the man who did that and beat him to death with his own hands. Wasn't hard to find the guy, he was living with the mother, and after he confessed, he told them that he couldn't help it, the little girl was always coming on to him. Shut up now, Carman had told him, shut up now or I'll kill you. Rolly took over, and they got him out, and the photographers were waiting when their car pulled up. Detectives Deshane and Menard arresting a suspect. He folded up the newspaper and put it back in one of the drawers, then got into bed.

He read for a while, a book about a plan to blow up an airliner, then turned out the light. It was late, but he didn't go to sleep. It was a warm night, the window open, a small screen in the gap. A car stopped. Voices. Carman lay listening to the night noises, the endless songs of frogs, high and low, the cry of a bird, a car far off, farther, a door opening, a hint of breeze, a barking dog, soft voices somewhere, a splash at the edge of the river, and behind it, faintly, the sound of the waterfall. The frogs went on and on. Did one stop and another begin, or was it the same ones, singing the whole night? Then among all these soft sounds, somewhere close by a woman cried out, and he was about to get up, to go and help, when he realized what he was hearing was a cry of pleasure. What sounded at first like suffering. Another and another. It didn't stop, little rhythmic details of articulation crossed the dark, throat music, panting breath. They must be out there on the lawn, next door, between his window and the river. If he went to the back window, he might be able to see them. It was what men and women did, and Amy had found herself a partner for the old song and dance. They didn't care if they were heard or seen. Or wanted to be. At the back window, he had watched her naked crossing the lawn, the long body and heavy breasts, and she had looked at him watching. Now her noise went on and on, and it worked in his nerves. Let them goddam keep it to themselves. The woman's moans and growls continued. Carman had never heard a woman go on like that. His failing, perhaps, that he had never brought a woman to such a protracted desperate extremity. It didn't stop as the minutes passed, and he put the pillow over his head not to hear it, though it made him feel he might suffocate.

And yet he soon slept, unconsciousness welling up to take him, and when he woke in the morning, the pale white curtains were full of sunlight, and far off a dog was barking. A car started and drove away. Carman climbed from bed, emptied his bladder and walked to the back window. Upstream, sunlight was glittering on the surface of the river, and even where the trees shaded the water, it had a sheen of light. Just to one side among the brilliant green spears of the grass, he saw a young rabbit, perfectly still, the soft quick ears almost translucent in the summer brightness. So nervous, so quick: all its safety was in the instantaneous snap of nerves. It had big dark frightened eyes. A sound or a movement startled it, and it was gone.

Norma on the nature of time: it passes. A time for this and a time for that. Et cetera. And so onward was how we assumed it went and would go. Once upon a time. Which time? The other time, the time of old stories. Once upon a time, a small child, she had climbed the stairs of her grandmother's house, a brick house on Victoria Street – every town had a Victoria Street – and she had walked into the room where her Aunt Sadie had died many years before, and as she stood in the room, she had felt the presence of her aunt, a thin nervous woman she had never liked, and the sense of that presence was so strong that for a long time, she could not draw herself away from it to go back down the stairs, and that night when they were sitting on the porch, watching the moths that flapped helplessly around the streetlight, she had tried to tell her grandmother, who thought she was talking about ghosts and didn't approve, but it wasn't ghosts, not altogether, but the inability to understand how a person could exist and then not exist. Years went on and more and more of them did it, started not existing, but she wasn't sure she understood that any better. Five years ago her friend Moira started not existing, and Norma still missed her. No one to argue with. One day Moira had been there, and the next, it seemed, she had never been there at all. Not that quick really, of course, but painful and protracted, and yet when you looked back, it was sudden and shocking. You could hear the voice in your head, but the phone wouldn't ring. It was no wonder they invented heaven and hell, easier to imagine that than the nothingness of nothing.

Norma remarked that this meditation on time was becoming a meditation on death. She closed her eyes and tried to listen to the flow of time. What she heard was the waterfall, time's interpreter, and the voices of boys shouting somewhere down by the river. Boys who would soon be men. On her lap lay a copy of *The Mill on the Floss*, which she had fished out to reread. She did that at least once a decade, read slowly through those wonderful pages where time was like time and yet without the sharp edges of unease. Like the Tullivers' mill, her house stood above the river, though here the mill itself was gone, the power of time no longer harnessed to active life. The river ran only because rivers ran. The cycle of rain and river and ocean and cloud went round and round. Then the river came into flood and Maggie died in her brother's arms, went back to a childhood before time was. Except she didn't go back except to nowhere, as if to the time before she existed. Into the pages of a book where time passed word by word and line by line, but you could look back and reconsider and so time never passed. Memory could look back across life, but couldn't reconsider, no, not really; the turned pages were turned. There were those who remembered an abduction by flying saucers and the strange beings who did things to them.

Time, you old gypsy man. Norma opened her eyes, stood up, belched mightily, farted daintily and decided to close the store for the day. A woman a few miles east wanted her to come and look at some things. She'd call and see if they could arrange to drive her out. If she bought anything, she'd hire Egan McBride to pick it up. She ought to have a car or a truck, but last year when her van crawled away to die, she didn't have the money to replace it, and she was trying to do without.

Carman found himself at the door of Norma's store, not wanting to be there, but there was no phone in the cottage, and he'd promised he'd get Carol a phone number in case she ever needed to know he was still alive. It was good of her to worry about him. He'd planned to ask Amy if he could give Carol her number, but then yesterday morning he'd seen her loading suitcases in the car, and she'd waved and shouted that she was moving. To live with a man. Well, judging by the noise he heard that night the man must be quite something. Why not go to him?

Now the cottage was empty, and he preferred it that way. In the dark he'd wakened suddenly and with the thought that there was someone near him or in the cottage next door, and for a moment he'd believed that it was Audrey, a confusion from his dreams. The mind, unattached to real things, got lost among the unreal ones. As a cop, you'd go to the door of an apartment high up in a building and an old woman would answer, and every question you asked made the eyes change, hide, go out of focus, and you knew that every question was an assault from a world that had been lost, that memory and television had carried the woman away so far that she couldn't come back to talk about whether she might have heard screams, whether she might have been looking out her window on the night in question, might have seen the events in the parking lot. You would have sworn that she had never known there was a parking lot, that there was nothing beyond the windows. She had gone inside and wouldn't come out. Trips to the grocery store were made with her eyes turned down to the pavement, not to see anything, to be safe. You asked her questions as carefully and as gently as you could, with the thought that perhaps just once she had looked out the window and remembered, but nothing came, and you thanked her and closed the door.

Norma was sitting in her usual place, the rocking chair near the back. The tape of birds was playing, and afternoon sunlight came in the back window and fell on the stuffed wolf which stood beside her chair, on guard. As usual she stared at him and didn't speak. Carman told himself that he wasn't going to get angry.

'I have to ask you a favour,' he said.

'You need your back scratched, like my friend here.' She

reached out and put her fingers in the wolf's hair and drew them back and forth.

Carman could feel the anger start, but he held it in check.

'I have a daughter in Toronto,' he said.

'What happened to your wife?' she said. 'You leave her for a sweet young thing?'

'She died.'

'I thought it was universal, taking off with a bimbo. My husband did it and now my son. Maybe it just runs in the family. Did she die recently?'

'A year and a half ago.'

She nodded, watched. He wished she'd stop staring at him like that, not saying anything.

'You shouldn't stare at people,' he said.

'Is that why you're so mad at the world, because she died?' she said.

'Could be.'

'A man who liked his wife,' she said. 'Put him in a museum. Last specimen extant. We should find who did my wolfy friend here and get you stuffed.'

He didn't tell her she was a crazy old bat; he had a favour to ask.

'My daughter wants a phone number. In case anything happens. I thought I could give her yours, if that's OK?'

'So she can phone every two days and send me down to see if you've had a stroke yet.'

'She won't likely phone. I keep in touch.'

She was staring again.

'I don't suppose I can say no to that. Filial piety and all. My son mostly tries to avoid me, though that's my own damn fault. I'm always rude to him.'

'Why's that?'

'Because he deserves it.'

'You're rude to everybody so far as I can see.'

'They all deserve it.'

Carman took out a pencil and paper.

'You'd better give me that number.'

She recited the seven digits, and he put them down.

'So Amy Martyrdom's moved out,' she said.

'Is that her name?'

'It's what I always called her. Suited.'

'She went this morning.'

'Finally found a man. I thought she'd probably have you in there before long.'

'A little old for her.'

'I don't know. What man could turn down tits like that? The way she told me, she was open to offers.'

'She talked to you about that?'

'Couldn't stop her.'

Carman put the pen and paper in his shirt pocket. Tonight he'd go to the pay phone by the garage and call Carol.

'About the phone,' he said. 'Thank you.'

She patted the wolf.

'What do you think I should ask for this?' she said.

'Damned if I know.'

'I'm getting attached to it. When I talk to it, it always looks interested. Can't say that for most.'

'Maybe you talk nicer to it.'

'That's true.'

A bell rang as the door of the shop opened and two men came in. They both had moustaches, short hair, shiny clean skin. Carman let himself out and walked down to the cottage.

At first she had no idea. She looked at the postcard in her hand, a picture of two buxom superheroes, one male and one female, on a background of exploding stars. On the back in careful printing, it said, *Did you buy the hotel? I saw one like it on a cowboy video. Love Luke.* It had an American stamp and was addressed to her with only her name, the town and the province, but it had arrived. The Post Office had its moods, and sometimes was unpredictably efficient. Luke. The boy in the middle of the night. Miss Virginia's son. She wondered if she ought to recognize the two unnatural figures that were bursting out of the sky, all tits and thighs. Male superheroes all had tits now – pectorals they were called.

The boy's printing was clear and almost elegant. She wondered where Miss Virginia had taken him now. She looked like a woman who knew too much, pretty, but everything strapped in place and lacquered. Even when she revealed her perfect body by sitting on the back dock in her bikini, it gave the impression of flesh that was under orders. The boy was polite and intelligent, even charming. The woman must be doing something right. Norma would have written a response to the card, but she had no address. The boy was gone, not to be seen again. A case of neverness.

She'd bought a bag of groceries at the general store which was at the top of the hill near the mailboxes. As she'd struggled up the steep street to the store, she'd wondered again what would become of her when she could no longer manage the climb. The Overholts, who owned it, were friendly enough people, and they might make a delivery now and then, but probably, once she couldn't make the climb, it would be time to move into town, to an apartment. Sit all day and watch television with the rest of the Golden Age Club.

A red sports car with the top open, what must be a vintage car by now, drove up the hill. Through the branches of the big maple that grew halfway down the hill overhanging the road, she watched the glitter of the upper river. When she was halfway down the hill she could see past the leaves and along the gravel road, and there was her tenant, The Vice-grip, doing something to the back steps of the cottage. Wood lay on the grass, and he was pounding nails. Fixing the back steps of the cottage. She'd never told him he could do that, or if she had she didn't remember, which amounted to the same thing. In fact she'd told him not to bother. Of course it was time it was done, but she was annoyed at his presumption. He should have asked politely, preferably hat in hand, and she might, with regal condescension, have given him permission to repair her property. Now he'd expect her to pay some vast sum for the wood. She knew the price of wood these days. He should mind his own damn business, but what man ever did?

Instead of taking her groceries home, she crossed the road.

Shook her fist at a small truck that tried to kill her on the way across. When she got close to the cottage, she looked at the neat piles of wood, the new framework with the first boards nailed across. It was cleanly done, but dammit he should have asked. He looked up and saw her but said nothing. He was wearing his criminal-on-the-run look, perhaps a result of cutting things up and pounding nails through them. She had herself noticed that driving in a nail could make one satisfyingly savage. Her ears rang as he drove one in.

'I suppose you're going to hand me a bill for this,' she said.

'No.' Bang, bang, bang.

'What?'

'I'm enjoying myself. But I wouldn't want to do too much of it.'

'But you want me to pay for the wood.'

'Don't bother. It wasn't all that much. I'm as glad to know I won't be breaking my leg.'

'It wasn't that bad,' she said.

He put another board in place and took nails from a small brown paper bag.

'Am I some kind of charity case?' she said. 'You think I can't pay my way.'

He didn't answer. The nerve of a barge horse, as her grandmother used to say. He pounded a nail. Bang, bang, bang.

'I don't need any favours,' she said, loudly over the noise of his hammering.

Bang, bang, bang. He ignored her.

'You never asked me if you could do this.'

'I said I'd fix it sometime.'

'And I said don't bother.'

'Is it better if I break my leg?'

He was hammering again.

'It's my cottage. If I want it repaired, I'll say so.'

'You're too late, and the stairs were dangerous.'

'How much did the wood cost?'

'It doesn't matter.'

'It damn well does matter.'

'I said I'd pay for it, didn't I?'

'And I said you wouldn't.'

He had the hammer raised over another nail.

'All right,' he said. 'I've got the receipt in my jacket pocket. I'll bring it over to the store.'

'You might as well give it to me right now.'

He stood up, the hammer still in his hand, and for a moment, Norma thought he might strike her down with it, but he put it down on the unfinished stairs, walked over to his car, took the jacket from the front seat, and pulled a piece of paper from the pocket. He came and gave it to her, and she was shocked at the total.

'You bought tools,' she said. 'You expect me to pay for those tools?' By now she was being completely unreasonable, and it pleased her.

'Deduct the tools,' he said. 'I'm sure you can do the arithmetic.'

Now he was being patient and long-suffering. It was a lucky thing she didn't have the hammer in her hand. She put the piece of paper into her shopping bag and turned to walk away. The pounding started again. By the time she got home and up the stairs to the kitchen, she was out of breath. No sooner had she sat down than the phone rang, and it proved to be the man's daughter wanting to leave him a message. Norma wasn't polite, but she wrote the message down. Maybe she could find someone to deliver it.

They'd finished dinner, and now they were sitting around the living room. The television was on, but nobody was watching. Carol was flipping through *Vanity Fair*, just looking at the pictures, and Grant had the *Globe and Mail Report on Business* and was going through the stock-market quotations with a pen, checking something off now and then. Grant had big ideas about money, but Carman didn't think he had the brains and the nerve to go with them. He'd always treated Carol well, and Carman liked him for that, but there was something about him that was soft and sad. Maybe if they had kids he'd grow into himself. The two of them did well enough. They got by. Grant managed a paint and wallpaper outlet, but he wasn't given a lot of freedom by the people who owned the chain. Carol was a receptionist in a big company office. It was one of those old-fashioned jobs for a woman, not the kind they were supposed to be getting these days. Sometimes she thought they might promote her to something better, but it didn't seem very likely.

They had car loans and a heavy mortgage on their little house near Dufferin and Bloor, a mortgage taken out when rates were high, and there wasn't a lot of slack in their budget. Carman wished he had more to help them out. When he sold the house, he gave them a piece of the cash. Carol said he shouldn't, but he told her she might as well have it now, not wait around for him to die. They'd done some repairs, paid off a big credit card bill, bought a dishwasher. When his heart finally blew up, there'd be some insurance money. That was about all he could do.

'Gold,' Grant said. 'Gold is always a good investment. Has been for thousands of years. You just have to get the right stock before everyone else.'

'I never followed the market,' Carman said. 'Never had the brains for it.'

He did what he could to discourage Grant, though probably nothing but losing money would do that. He only hoped it wouldn't be too much.

'Hasn't she got an incredibly beautiful face?' Carol said. She was holding up the picture of some actress. He knew he should recognize her, but he didn't.

'A lot of it's done by the photographer.' He said that, but there was something about the face that was naked and riveting. A world of beautiful women promising perfection, but nobody ever brought it home. What happened was something different. Sometimes he thought that being a cop had ruined him. You always got called when people were at their worst. The things they hid from the world, the cops got to see. Most of what you heard was lies. You saw blood and rage and the way people could convince themselves that whatever they did was right. Someone took away the bodies, and you tried to make sure that your notebook was accurate and complete so that you didn't have a lawyer make a fool of you in court. If necessary, you lied. The old system was to grab the most likely suspect and beat a confession out of him, and it worked. If you didn't do it yourself, you knew others who did. You said it didn't bother you, and you were afraid that might be true. At the end you got a pension.

'I've been reading up on some of these technology stocks,' Grant said. 'There's money to be made in them. The new economy.'

Carman wanted to go over and shake him a few times, to wake him up, shout at him that he wasn't a bright guy and he should catch on to that. He got up from his chair. Carol was still looking at the photograph of that hauntingly beautiful face as if by staring at it, she could find herself looking like that. She wasn't a bad-looking girl. A photographer like that could make something of her too. What she'd always wanted. To be a model. To be someone the camera loved.

'Time for me to go,' he said.

'Don't rush off,' Carol said. 'Stay and watch *Seinfeld*.'

'You know me,' he said. 'I get restless. I'll come back another time. Or you can come and visit me.'

'Is that place all right? The cottage?'

'Yeah. You should come out sometime. I'll take you fishing.'

Carman had bought himself a cheap rod and some worms from the general store and had fished a little from the dock and caught a couple of perch. He was planning to take the boat out when he got back the next day.

'I don't know why you didn't keep the apartment,' Carol said.

'I didn't like it. Ten floors up, locked in a little box. Not for me.'

Carol hugged him, and Grant shook his hand, and he left. When he got in the car, he took a few deep breaths and checked his pulse, just to prove he was still alive. Then he started back. The long summer daylight hung in the sky over the city as he drove across Dundas toward the Don Valley Parkway. There was a crowd outside the Eaton Centre watching a busker juggling. A young guy with the exaggerated arms and shoulders of a bodybuilder stood on the next corner, dressed in tight jeans and a tank top, advertising himself; he was watching a well-dressed woman in a pale fawn suit and carrying a briefcase as she walked by him. Carman caught a red light at Church, and while he was waiting he saw a girl get out of a low black car. It was the young hooker he'd taken out to the motel. She was wearing the same shorts and sequined T-shirt. Working clothes. She looked around her, as if she was searching for someone, walked a few steps, turned and walked back. Meeting a friend, a pimp, a john. She couldn't stand still. The light changed. Carman looked at the young pretty legs as he moved away into the traffic, toward the highway, and as he drove through the oncoming darkness, he could remember the little breasts she'd shown him, her edginess, the way she moved on high heels. She had brought off dozens of men since that night, in parked cars down an alleyway or rented rooms, a trail of used condoms left behind her. Maybe one day she'd walk away from the life, or maybe not. If you thought about it, she was a beautiful girl, but she'd never have the brains to see it.

As a young cop on the beat, he'd wondered about hookers, what they thought about while some man was using them for a toilet, but then you saw a hundred more of them, and you stopped wondering. They were as impersonal as cab drivers; they got the customer where he wanted to go then picked up another fare.

The lights of the car reached out along the night highway. Carman kept his foot down. Somewhere in the night, a young animal might run into the glare of the lights and go under the wheels. Staring into the darkness, the opposing headlights flashing into his eyes, he thought he saw that young girl, thin and naked, caught in his headlights, her mouth open trying to say something to him. Carman shook his head to rouse himself and opened the window to let the cool night air roar over him. There was a headache starting behind his eyes.

By the time he got to the village, driving past Norma's store, which had a light on in one of the upstairs windows, turning down the gravel road and into the driveway, he was so tired that at first he couldn't get out of the car, and for several minutes he sat there, unable to move, his legs and back aching, feet swollen and tight inside his shoes, his head pounding, but he knew he must get himself inside, and he opened the car door, stood for a minute holding on, listening to the frogs, the waterfall, some distant music, then he got himself up the back stairs and into the house. He sat on the edge of the bed to pull off his shoes and trousers and shirt, then rolled in and pulled the covers over him.

It was early when he woke, and from the bed he could see an irregular patch of sunlight falling on the kitchen floor, shimmering with a pattern of blown leaves. He was still tired, but he wanted to be out on the river, and he got himself up and took a quick shower, drank a glass of juice, and picked up the oars, the fishing pole and the box of worms from under the cottage. One afternoon he'd dragged the boat down to the water, and now it was tied to the dock front and back, the nose into the weeds at the edge of the river. He laid rod and worms on the dock and climbed down into the boat, which rocked heavily, then reached down the pole and oars, set the oars in place, untied the two ropes and pushed off, the boat floating quickly out from his last push and starting to drift in the current as he took his place and took the first pull on the oars. He rowed easily, not pushing himself, just using slow strokes to propel himself upstream past the other cottages. At the last cottage, a woman was cutting the lawn with an old hand mower, and she waved to him. She'd introduced herself one day, but he couldn't remember her name. He waved to her and dipped the oars. With a look over his shoulder, he checked the slight bend in the river and turned the bow of the boat to follow it. Ahead he could see the old railway bridge. Sometimes on weekends, kids played on the bridge, jumping from it into the deep water below. Halfway to the bridge there was a thick branch of an old willow leaning close to the water, and he planned to tie the boat there.

Beside him, a large dragonfly hovered over the shining surface of the water on its transparent wings, then flew upward and out of sight. The sun was shining on his back, and he liked the sensation of warmth. He felt the bow of the boat bump against the willow branch, and he turned, caught some of the leaves, then the branch itself, and shifted on the seat to reach the rope and tie it. He should get some kind of anchor for the boat. Then he could drop anchor and fish anywhere on the river.

There was a small silver spinner on the line, and he fastened a worm on the hook behind it and cast the lure downriver, let it sink through the water, then began to reel it in, very slowly, feeling the pull of the current again the line. The river reflected the blue sky and in the shallows the round green leaves of the waterlilies floated on the surface, two white flowers floating among them, but the depths of the river were a deep brown like clear coffee. Somewhere down there, the fish moved in their cold place. Within the skeleton they had an extra sense to read the movements of the current, and the muscles of the long thin bodies made them quick and efficient through the flowing water. They hunted and slept in the filtered light of day and in the shapely fluid darkness, quick and simple and persistent.

He lifted the lure from the water and cast again, the weight of it pulling the line evenly off the reel, dropping with a small slap into the water as he turned the handle of the reel once to engage the drag, then waited as the lure sank glittering into the invisible depth of the river and finally began to draw it back. A patient kind of suspense, the fingers attentive for a change in the action of the line. Audrey might be back at the cottage, expecting him. Wasn't. The boat floated in the middle of a great emptiness. Sunlight. Birdsong. The trains no longer arrived here. The hotel was boarded up. He cast and retrieved.

When the sudden tug on the line came he was astonished, as if he'd forgotten there was any point to this activity except the waiting. He snapped the rod up and began to reel in the line. The rod bent and the tight line ran through the water as the fish tried to escape, then it came upward, and the fish jumped into the light, then dropped again, and he drew it in, saw it at the side of the boat and lifted it carefully aboard. A bass, green and fierce-looking, the tail flapping against the bottom of the boat. It was long and thick-bodied, and he decided that he would keep it and eat it for dinner. A lot of the fish were full of chemicals these days. Carcinogens. He laughed out loud at the thought. He wouldn't be around for the cancer to get him. He unhooked the fish, broke its neck and left it in the bottom of the boat as he baited the hook again. Anything more he caught he'd put back.

He watched the sunlight catch ripples made by the current as it ran against the side of the boat, little folds of water reflecting the light. The air was full of quiet sounds that made you feel the silence behind them.

Norma had decided to be good the next time she saw Carman Deshane, though she had to admit he brought out the worst in her. Well, bad temper, whether that was the worst or not. Maybe it was the best. It kept her going. She'd been an old bitch over the porch stairs, she knew that, but she didn't like surprises, and she didn't like men taking things over without telling her. She'd worked out what she owed him for the wood and had it sitting in an envelope, and someday when she was feeling good she'd take a walk down to the cottage and deliver it to him. She was supposed to be taking a look at Amy Martyrdom's place as well, just to see if it was all right. Amy had called her from the city to ask her to do that and had mailed her the key. She was still paying the rent, not trusting her new happiness too far. Smarter than she looked. When she called she wanted to tell Norma everything about her sex life, but after a couple of minutes Norma cut her off. Put A into B, fold C over D etc. People did get worked up about it, she had herself now and then, but hearing someone boast about her orgasms over the telephone was nobody's idea of a good time.

Sometimes Norma was tempted to call Aeldred, who was her last lover and was probably available, his most recent wife gone they said, but she held a grudge and besides she mostly felt too lousy.

As if summoned up by her thoughts of him, The Retired Vice-grip pulled up in front, got out of his car and approached the door of the shop. She reached into the desk drawer for the envelope of money, and by the time he came in, she was on her way to meet him. She held it out.

'For the wood,' she said.

He held the envelope in his hand for a second, as if he was thinking something, but she couldn't read his face. Then he put the envelope in his pocket. Warm as it was outside, he was wearing a tweed jacket.

'You have any scrap metal?' he said.

'Now that's not a question I was expecting.'

'Do you?'

'If I get any, it mostly goes to Spare Parts.'

'Where's that?'

'A sculptor. Josef Ancil is his name, but he has a big sign on his studio from an old garage. Says Spare Parts, so most of us call him that.'

'What's he want with scrap metal?'

'Builds things out of it. Very nice, some of them. I've got a little one upstairs. Made out of the blade of an old plow welded together with some bolts and a couple of other things.'

He ignored that as something of no interest.

'I'm looking for an anchor for the boat. I thought you might have something around I could buy from you, something heavy and not too big.'

'Why do you need an anchor?'

'Fishing.'

'You always been a fisherman?'

'Not for years.'

'Catch anything?'

'Yes. A few bass, a pike. Surprised me.'

'Josef would likely have something, if you feel like a drive.'

'All right.' She'd expected that he'd hum and haw and say no. Surprise.

'Don't suppose it's good business to take off whenever I feel the need, but I enjoy it.'

At the front door, she turned the sign. Closed. A firm satisfying word.

In the car, she turned down the window and laid her arm on the edge to give the sun a chance to start a little cancer. She hadn't been to see Spare Parts for a long time, and she was looking forward to the long shed full of odd assemblages of old metal, and a few of wood. Most of the wood was roughed out with an adze but now and then he'd get hold of hardwood and turn out a piece with a high polish. The metal piece in her living room was something she'd got in trade for some ancient squared walnut that she'd picked up a few years back. Spare Parts had taken one look and decided that he must have it, and after a lot of negotiation, she'd made the trade. She was out of pocket, but the sculpture had given her enough pleasure to justify that.

The road ran down a hill, and close to a lake, and in the distance she saw a boat on the water, and then it disappeared behind a stand of spruce. You could imagine so many things taking place behind those trees. A few miles further, they came to the turnoff and drove along a gravel county road that twisted between snake fences and patches of bush. There was almost no soil over the rock here, and the fields were full of wild grasses with patches of blue burr and purple vetch, yellow butter-and-eggs close to the ground, daisies and black-eyed Susans. A thousand flowers. Millefleur. The tapestry of waste land, logged and abandoned. They went around a turn, and she saw the big sign in old-fashioned lettering. Spare Parts. The house was a low nineteenth-century limestone with white trim, mullioned windows six over six, well kept up. Josef was usually to be found in the workshop, a tidy frame building attached to the long log shed where he stored wood and metal and some of the completed pieces that hadn't sold.

In front of the shed was a big garden, neatly planted, a few rows of tall corn, tomatoes that hung, round and pale green, among the dark green leaves, hills of squash and cucumbers, rows of beets and beans. Spare Parts had a girlfriend in town who came out for a weekend now and then and helped him with the garden, but he was a bugger to work and probably would have kept everything perfect even without her. Looking at his sturdy muscular body, watching the slow steady way he worked, it made you understand why God had troubled to invent the male.

Carman was parking the car at the end of the lane. Spare Parts, his welding mask pushed up from his face, came out of the door of the workshop and stood under the big sign, staring at the car to see who was arriving. Norma waved to him. He nodded, almost smiled.

'My friend here is looking for an anchor for his boat, Josef. I said you had the best collection of scrap metal in Eastern Ontario.'

He nodded and pointed to a pile of junk just inside the door of the log shed. Carman walked over to it, looked down for a minute and took out a piece that looked like a large flat doughnut. He hefted it to check the weight.

'How much do you want for that?' he said.

Spare Parts, not a great one for talk, held up five fingers. He had short heavy hands that looked as if they'd have no skill at all, but he could do anything with them. Norma watched him as the other man found his wallet and took out a bill. Josef had a tight, almost mean-looking face, very concentrated and closed, but if you got him to speak, he was bright and even funny. He took the bill and shoved it in his pocket.

'All right if we look around the shed?'

He nodded and went back into the workshop. Norma made her way to the wide shed doorway while Carman put his anchor away in the truck. She stood in the centre of the floor and looked around her. A couple of pieces were oddly unbalanced and wrong. Maybe they weren't finished, or maybe she just didn't understand them. Another used the curving teeth of an old harrow to make something that looked at if it might fly, an organic, insect look to it. A pile of steel T-bars lay against a wooden box, and behind them was a geometric form like a crazed jungle gym. When Arthur was little they'd had something like that in the yard, but all symmetrical and with none of the delight of this.

'You like this junk?'

She turned to look at him, didn't like the look on his face any better than what he'd said.

'Yes.'

'You call this sculpture?'

'I do.'

'If I fastened a lot of junk together, would that be sculpture?'

'Depends how well you did it.'

'How could you tell?'

'How can you tell Donatello from Canova?'

'Never heard of either one.'

'So what the hell do you know about it?'

'Not a lot.'

'Then don't advertise your ignorance.'

She could see the face grow still, the life withdraw from the eyes, and she looked at the pile of steel T-bars behind him and knew that he was very close to breaking her head with one of them. Not to encourage him, she turned and walked away. The window of the workshop was bright with the blue glare of Josef's arc-welding torch, joining metals by the transforming anger of electricity, Josef behind a mask to keep his eyes safe from the brilliance at the point of fusion.

She heard footsteps behind her and waited for the steel bar to come down and break her skull, but they went toward the door of the shed and away. Maybe he'd drive off in the car and leave her here. If so she'd beg Spare Parts for a ride. Damn fool deserved everything she'd said to him and more. She wouldn't tolerate stupidity. No doubt one of the reasons that Steven had left, having found some adoring little thing who'd tell him he was a genius and had the biggest dick she'd ever seen. Stupidity was endless.

In the corner of the shed was a mobile made from thin curled pieces of metal, painted white and dark red. She went toward it to study it more closely, as Carman took his murderous look back to the car. The mobile was a beautiful thing. Calder's idea, of course, that such a thing might be. Spare Parts was good, but not a giant. Would you know if you met a giant? A sign on the forehead, Genius at Work. Sorry but I'm busy creating *The Rite of Spring*.

New things, unheard-of until now; the modern is very up to date. Norma wasn't. She went missing somewhere just west of Mark Rothko. Assuming The Vice-grip waited for her, she could tell him about colour field paintings on the way back. He'd be sure to enjoy that. Idiot. No doubt the wife had been the same, TV and recipes clipped from magazines. She couldn't even imagine the daughter. Whereas her son Arthur could be boasted of as one of the supreme bores of our time. Now that was an accomplishment.

She looked toward the car. He was sitting in the driver's seat, waiting. Well, he'd got his anchor, hadn't he? and he should be used to her temper by now. If he didn't want to make her mad, he shouldn't behave stupidly.

Carman lay in bed and listened to the sound of rain on the roof. He'd planned to go out fishing this morning, but when he woke, he heard the rain and changed his mind. Fishing was supposed to be good in the rain, but he wasn't going to bother. So he lay in bed and heard the soft reiterating sound over his head and dozed and thought about things. Lately he'd taken to remembering men he'd met on the streets. That junkyard reminded him of Billy McTeer. Billy had a store that sold a bit of everything, including stolen goods. On one side of it, appliances, on the other car parts, and in between some furniture. Jewellery in the back counter. After a few months of playing games, threats, promises, hints, Billy became Carman's best informant, and it was a long time before Carman realized that he didn't do it because he had to or because he was scared of the police; he liked turning people in. Enjoyed the act of betrayal. Every time he gave Carman information, his long face would take on a funny smile, and he'd give Carman a big wink. Then one day Billy didn't open the store, and nobody ever heard from him again. He'd talked once too often. Nobody spent a lot of time worrying about who had got rid of him. It was one of the hazards of what he did. Carman missed him, but not much.

Carman couldn't do this before, lie in bed in the morning, lazy and useless, his thoughts drifting. It must be the river close by that calmed him. When he got up, he'd make coffee and sit by the window to watch the pattern of raindrops on the surface, then he'd have toast and watch some more. Later on he'd go up to the pay phone to call Carol and invite them out for a weekend. The cottage was small, but they had a tent, and if the weather was good they could put it up in the yard. He'd get a little barbecue and some charcoal and they could cook some steaks. Carol would like that. She enjoyed those storybook things. Since Amy left, the yard was always quiet and private, a cedar hedge on one side, an empty yard on the other.

If the rain stopped, he'd walk up to the general store for some groceries. He liked the two teenage kids who worked there, a brother and sister, niece and nephew of the Overholts, smart and pleasant both of them, same body shape with short heavy legs, same perfect teeth. At first he wondered if they were twins, but the boy was older.

When he woke this morning he'd been dreaming about Audrey. In the dream he knew that she was supposed to be dead, and there was something about her skin, grey and porous, that suggested the skin of a corpse. Every day when he sat by the back window, her eyes in the picture watching him, he struggled to understand what death was, how she could have been here, looking just like that picture, but now was gone. Amy, his neighbour, was gone, but he could find her. Norma talked to her on the phone sometimes. A car might pull up and she would climb out, her big breasts in front of her; she might even move back into the cottage, slip out through the darkness to swim, but Audrey wasn't at the end of any electronic circuit, and she wouldn't come back. They used to believe that the dead were in some other world, that we could die and join them; you could understand how people wanted to believe all that.

A gust of wind blew rain against the bedroom window, and it began to fall more noisily on the roof, the drumming faster. On the back lawn there would be a robin searching for worms. Tomorrow the hot sun would draw back the water that had fallen, taking water vapour high into the air to form new clouds, which would be carried around the world, and in some other country, rain would fall.

The Day of the Bad Habit. Putting It into Words. Her Kind of Foolishness.

Some days her mind did tricks like that; everything turned into the title of an imaginary book. The Chapters of Common Life. The Table and Chair Suite. Other People's Kitchens. The Business of Failure. Waiting for Cash. Sun of the Summer Mornings. The Day after Insomnia. The Closed and Open Shop. Cars That Pass, Cars That Stop. Life on the Radio. Dances for Aging Bones. The Long Comfort of Chairs. Double Entry Bookkeeping for Amateurs. The Book of Numbers. How to Repair China. Tacks, Taxes and Taxidermy. The Age of Antiques. Antiquity Unsung.

Unsuitable Activities for Unstable Seniors.

The Weasel's Little Teeth.

Quandaries for the Quaint.

Xenophon on the Xylophone.

How Dumb Can You Get.

The Long Comfort of Chairs. Riversound. The Taste of Morning Coffee. Cars That Pass, Cars That Stop. The Day after Insomnia. Sun of the Summer Mornings. The Suddenly Coming Customer. You Just Never Know.

Lost Mica Mines. The Tourist's Question and Other Disappointments. Doing Your Best Anyway. Forced Smiles. Mother Taught Me Manners.

Giving Directions. The Short Goodbye. The Kindly Chairseat. The River That Runs Forever. Just Another Day. The Tenant Passeth By. Retired Vice-grips and Other Questions of Conscience. The Rented Cottage and the Empty Cottage. Exodus. Martyrdom Wins Out. Amy in the Rough Arms of Love.

The Waterfall Goes On and On. Summer Days and Winter Nights. Thoughts of Lunch. The Common Sandwich. The Gospel According to Mustard. Hypnagogic Dancers. Goodbye, Hello, I'm Here. Cars That Stop, Cars That Pass. The Long Summer Afternoon. Small Sales and Making Change. A Book to Read, a

Book to Sell. The Question of Traffic. A Walk to the Post. The Epistle of Arthur. Motherhood for Crabby Dames. The Waterfall Goes On and On. Toward the Close of Day. The Open and Closed Shop. Symptoms of Living. The Food We Eat. Mosquito Harvest. Lessons for Nightfall. A Prayer to the Absent. Last Words.

The water was black, heavy and shining like oil as he moved the boat toward the shore, which fell away from him as he propelled the boat with long strokes of the oars. Then he was moving ahead, and he knew that the dock was close by, and the boat slithered into the mud at the edge of the black water, embedding its prow in the weeds and slop, and he knew that he would sink into the mud as he tried to climb ashore, but the dock was almost in reach, so he stretched his arm and caught hold of a corner of it and pulled the boat near enough that he could clamber up. He knew that he should tie the boat, but it was taking all his strength to get to the dock. He would have to abandon the boat. Once on the dock, he had to step carefully down to the lawn, and it took a long time to cross toward the house. It was hard to lift his feet. A light was on in the house, and he could see someone reading by the window, thought that it must be Audrey waiting for him, but as he came a little closer, forcing his legs to bear him, he saw that at the cottage next door, the back door was wide open, though it was almost dark inside, only a hint of something like candlelight. She had left the door open for him, and he knew that she was waiting. He stopped pushing his way through the long grass and studied the open door, the gaping darkness, and then turned and struggled toward it. He could no longer see Audrey reading by the window.

Once he was inside the cottage, he spoke, called out her name, but there was no answer, and he was aware that the long hall led to a number of rooms, and he could see that in each room a candle was burning, but when he looked inside, no one was there, until he came to the last room, which had no candle, only a little light that seeped in through the doorway, but when he reached the door, something was blocking the light and he could hardly see. Amy was lying on the floor, her long thin legs spread to show a dark bush of hair. He knew that he had come too late, and that she was dead. She had been waiting for him, but it had taken too long for him to row the boat to shore and to cross the lawn. Now he didn't know what to do. He could feel the hot pressure of his desire for her, but you couldn't do that to a dead woman, but still he found himself releasing his clothes and lying on her, and as he did he saw her face form a smile and the eyes opened, and then he was on his knees looking at her, and she was covered with blood.

He woke, shaken by the dream, the taint of blood lingering in the mind. Outside, the sun was shining brightly, and he heard voices. Carol and Grant were already awake and down at the river. He could hear them splashing in the water. Last night Carol insisted that she was going to get him in the water today. He told her he had no bathing suit, and she said they'd drive into Kingston and get him one. In fact he had a pair of old Bermuda shorts that Audrey once bought him that he could wear to swim, but he didn't think he would.

Once up and washed, he took the bottle of drinking water out of the fridge and filled the kettle. Apparently some of the people in the cottages drank the river water, but he wasn't going to. He watched from the window as Carol dived off the dock. The water was too shallow to dive, and he nearly went to the door and shouted at her. Hard to remember that she was grown up. Probably she didn't mind him fussing a little. She knew it was a sign of affection. She knew that he'd be lost if anything happened to her; she was the last thing left to him. They'd only had the one child. Audrey had a hard time of it in childbirth, and there wasn't a lot of money, so they postponed having a child for a few years, and then tried for a year without success, and by then it seemed too late. They had Carol, and they both loved her, and that was enough. Every time a report came into the station about a kid missing, Carman found himself phoning home to make sure that Carol was all right. It was superstitious, but he had to do it. He saw too much of how uncertain things were, kids lost, kids run over.

Carol had bought a new bathing suit, yellow and bright green.

It made her skin look pale. She said that this afternoon she was going to lie on the dock and get a tan, and Grant reminded her about skin cancer. Carman wanted to scoff, but he knew that Grant was right. Or thought he knew. If the scientists knew what they were talking about. They sometimes did. What a world, when the sun had grown dangerous.

When the kettle boiled, he made a pot of coffee and got out the sweet buns he'd bought at a bakery a few miles away. He'd got those and a little hibachi and charcoal, steaks and a couple of bottles of wine. They drank the first one last night after they arrived. Carol insisted that today they were going to see Norma's store. She was sure she'd find something valuable on sale cheap, though he'd warned her that Norma would just stare at her and be rude. Maybe she wouldn't. Maybe it was Carman set her off.

They'd sat out on the lawn last night, drinking wine until the mosquitoes drove them in, and Carman had whittled away at a piece of the pine left over from the stairs, making himself a float to use fishing in the deep water above the dam. He wasn't sure it would work, but he was going to try it.

Carol had looked across at him as he carved the wood.

'I've never seen you do anything like that before,' she said.

'Never had so much time on my hands.'

'You going to catch fish to feed us?'

'Maybe. I'm not sure they're not full of chemicals. All right for me, but you still have years ahead of you.

'All that pollution,' Grant said. 'You'd think they'd do something about it.'

'Not much to be done by now,' Carman said.

They sat in silence drinking their wine, and soon the mosquitoes came.

Now Carman went out the back door and shouted to them that he had coffee made, and they picked up their towels and rubbed themselves dry. As he turned to go back in, he looked at the empty cottage next door and remembered the dream, the naked bleeding body. The brain so full of strange things. He poured himself a glass of juice and took two pills. Last night before dinner, his chest had been bad, and he'd had to put two of the nitroglycerin capsules under his tongue before it eased, but he'd managed to do it without Carol noticing. No point worrying her. Now he put the plate of buns on the table, two wineglasses full of juice, and three mugs for coffee. Carol and Grant came in the back door, both with T-shirts pulled on over their bathing suits. Grant's shirt had SUPERSALESMAN written on the front. Carol's was long, almost as long as a mini-dress.

'This is such a great place,' Carol said. 'How did you find it?'

'Accident. I was wandering around back roads and I ended up here. Saw the sign in the store window.'

'When you told us about it, it sounded crazy, but I can see why you wanted it.'

'I like the river.'

'Are you going to go swimming with us?'

'We'll see.'

'You're a good swimmer, aren't you?'

'No. Your mother was. I can stay afloat.'

'Didn't she once win medals for swimming?'

'That's right.'

'I bet the land around here's a good investment,' Grant said.

'Why?'

'It's a nice place. One of these days it will get developed.'

'Could be.'

Carol was pouring coffee for them all.

'Shall we tell him?' she said to Grant. A kid with a secret.

'Sure.'

Carol looked at him.

'We decided last night not to wait any longer. To have a baby.'

Carman walked away from the table. Sudden tears in his eyes at the thought of this baby, the memory of how Audrey had wanted grandchildren, and at the same time, he knew in some terrible way that he wouldn't be around to see it. He knew it, though he wanted not to. By the time he'd got the milk out of the fridge and put the bottle on the table, he had control of himself.

'That sounds like a pretty good idea.'

'Is that all you have to say?'

'It's a great idea, but if it's a boy, don't name it after me. I never liked the name Carman.'

'I never much liked my own name either,' Grant said. 'I wonder who does?'

'I like mine just fine,' Carol said.

'When you were a kid, you always wanted some fancier name,' Carman said. 'Candace was one you liked.'

'I don't remember that.'

'We would have called you Candy,' Grant said.

'Two for a nickel,' Carol said. 'Look, what's that, that blue bird?'

'A kingfisher. I see them all the time.'

'It moves so fast.'

'The field down below the waterfall is full of goldfinches.'

'What are they like?'

'Wild canaries. Yellow and black.'

Carol stood by the window with her cup of coffee, staring down at the river.

'I always thought I was a city girl, and I never thought I'd like a summer cottage, but I see why people have them.'

'We had cottages in the summer a couple of times.'

'All I remember is being bored. For me the best holiday was when we went to New York.'

'Drove me nuts. Crazy drivers. Crazy people. Dirt on the streets.'

'We thought we might go to New York for Christmas this year,' Grant said.

'You're welcome to it.'

Carman poured himself a second cup of coffee, though he knew he shouldn't. They were young, planning ahead, while he was always startled to wake in the morning and find he was still alive. The way it was, must be, should be perhaps, if you thought all this hodgepodge of living had a meaning and necessity. He had spent years enforcing the laws, and that was right, though maybe hopeless. You put one kid in jail, and the next was in a corner of the schoolyard kicking the shit out of someone smaller than he was, getting ready for the next step. The world was as it was. The cops kept a closer eye on a factory if the owner handed out bottles of rum at Christmas time. You never thought of that as corruption, just good manners.

Carol turned from the window and looked at him, and for a second he thought that she knew what he was thinking.

'Can we come back some other weekend?'

'Whenever you want.'

Grant was at the table glancing through an out-of-date newspaper.

'If you want to go fishing,' Carman said, 'we could get a couple of cheap poles at the general store.'

'You two go,' Carol said. 'I'll amuse myself.'

When the young woman walked into the shop, Norma didn't know who she was. The friendly smile on her face made it clear that Norma was supposed to recognize her, and an attempt was made, futile at first and then, just before the girl was going to have to introduce herself Norma recognized the face, and still unable to come up with the name, indicated that she wasn't entirely at sea by asking if Arthur was parking the car and was then perfectly astonished to find that the woman was on her own. I just thought I'd come and see you was the line.

She stood there, bold as you please, smiling. Norma finally remembered her name. Julie. There was nothing for it but to be friendly, so Norma sent her back to the door to lock it and put up the Closed sign, and the two of them went upstairs, Norma doing her best to be spry and light-footed and disguise the pains in her back and legs. When it became obvious that she was being watched, she told the girl about her imaginary dumb waiter, and the girl made a show of amusement. Possibly was amused.

Upstairs, Norma boiled water, dug out stale biscuits, set them on the table beside the old cigar box full of sheets of mica, which for some reason she'd dragged up here a couple of weeks ago. Left on the table because she didn't know what else to do with it.

'How's Arthur?' she said, for lack of anything better to say.

'He's worried about his father.'

'Why's that?'

'Steven's had a couple of mild strokes recently. Once when he was having dinner with us, he couldn't talk for ten minutes. He went to lie down for a while, and then he was OK. Another time he fell and the doctor said it was probably another stroke. He's taking medication, but there could be another one any time.'

Norma thought about it, Steven silent and helpless. Felt nothing much except the awareness of general mortality that dogged her days and would. She set the tea on the table.

'Is that why you're here?' she said.

'I guess so. I wanted to talk to you again, and I thought it was something you might like to know.'

'Why?'

'You were together for quite a while. You had a child together.'

'Where's the bimbo?'

'She moved to Vancouver a few years ago. She was offered a good job out there.'

'Steven's on his own.'

'Yes.'

'And you expect me to go running back and help him through a difficult old age, wipe his ass when he gets incontinent and hold his hand while he's dying?'

'No. Nothing like that. I've been mad at a man who betrayed me. I know you don't get over it. But I thought you might want to write or give him a call. Mostly I thought you'd like to know.'

Norma poured tea.

'Yes, I suppose I do like to know, though I couldn't honestly say I care a lot.'

The younger woman met her eyes, and Norma realized that she'd been staring. It was a bad habit and got worse. Privilege of age, to indulge your bad habits freely. For a while they were silent, drinking tea, crunching dry biscuits. Country hospitality, more or less. Norma could feel her stomach growling. Other growls to come close behind.

'Does all this mean that you're serious about Arthur?'

'Yes.'

'Lucky Arthur. Don't you find him a little … heavy?'

The eyes met hers, surprised.

'I mean mentally. Humourless.'

'He has quite a nice sense of humour when he's relaxed.'

'I don't suppose he's ever relaxed around here.'

'Parents and children. They set each other off.'

Norma finished her tea. She was mostly annoyed by this attempt at friendliness. The girl was trying to remind Norma of a time before she was a bear rumbling in its cave, sharp claws, querulous temper, as if there was such a time, before the pelt was matted and torn, the old bear fat and slow from too many grubs and berries. As if there was such a time. Christmas-card scenes, the three of them sitting by the fire, Norma and Steven watching over Arthur as he builds complicated machines with an old-fashioned Meccano set inherited from his loving father. Norma has made cookies and the parents drink their tea and eat macaroons while they admire the talents of their son, and outside the cold snow falls, but they are safe from it. It must have happened, things like that. They were a family once, and Arthur had been a bright and loving boy. Norma sat on the edge of the bed and read him books, something about a duck. As if there was such a time. The bear shifted its heavy shoulders, sniffed the dark.

Norma looked at the younger woman who sat across from her. She looked proud of herself, the dark eyes shining in the square blunt face. A few months in Arthur's bed and she thought she had the right to poke the old bear with a stick and rouse it, drive it down the road, make it dance, would be shocked if she found bleeding claw marks on her face. She thought that what she was doing was love, correctness, a helping hand. Incorrigibly stupid like all her race.

'If you ever wanted to see him, I could drive you.'

'That's all gone by. Steven made his bed. Made mine too. Time was I wept to have him back, while he was pumping the bimbo into seventh heaven. I can't even remember him now.'

She had no idea whether or not that was true. She had a momentary image of the dark curling hair on his chest, his red mouth, but that was a young man, not an old one. What terrible hungry sentimentality had driven this girl to come to Norma when she might have stayed away? What evil corruption of the imagination that she would have called love? Norma would have no more of that. She would be preserved from the well-meaning.

'You're probably right,' the woman said. 'I shouldn't have interfered.'

Norma looked toward her, and there was a candour in her look, and something subtle and real. Needing a response, having none, she took the box of mica that lay on the table in front of her and pushed it toward the girl.

'Take this,' she said. 'It's not worth anything.'

'What is it?'

'Mica, from one of the old mines.'

The girl opened the box, and her small thick fingers took out a small sheet of the mineral and held it up. The light caught it and shone silver and gold. One of the thin sheets slid off the top of the piece and broke. She swept it up with her fingers and put it back in the box.

'Are you giving this to me?'

'I found it in my storage room. I can't remember where it came from. They used to mine it near here.'

'What for?'

'Electrical insulators. Some of it was used in stoves. Or they ground it up to make industrial fillers.'

Julie took another piece and sat with it in the palm of her hand.

'You go back to Arthur and make him happy,' Norma said. 'You've done your best.'

When Julie looked at her now, she was different, older, as if everything up until this moment had been a performance, a pretence of youth and innocence. Now her face was that of a woman of no particular age, who knew what there was to know, the earth smell of the bear's den where Norma passed the long winter, the itch of ticks, the anger at being poked and prodded. They were simple female animals, watching.

Julie took up the box, turned away from the table and walked down the stairs without saying a word.

A couple of days of rain, and now the heavy August heat. By the river there was some freshness, but if he walked as far as the store, Carman was bathed in sweat, found it running into his eyes, and he would keep trying to wipe it away with his arm, but the arm was damp with sweat as well. He'd bought some iced-tea mix at the store, and he mostly sat in the shady part of the yard with a glass of iced tea. Even in the middle of the day, he sometimes found he was dozing off, though at night he'd lie in bed with one sheet over him, trying to keep the dark thoughts away. You'd hear a single mosquito in the dark and wait for it to come close enough that you could swat it. He'd swat his arm or shoulder where he felt the tingling presence, and the tiny noise would start up again, letting him know that he'd missed the insect and wondering whether to turn on the light and get up to find and kill it.

That was one good thing about the high apartment in the city. The bugs never got up that high. Maybe the only good thing. If it cooled a little in the evening, he thought he might take the boat out and fish for a while. It had been too hot for the last week, but now and then a breeze would come up in the evening. He thought of the fish in their sunken world where the heat of the sun was filtered by tons of water, and it was always deep and cold, though if he stepped in the shallows by the dock to cool himself, he was aware that even the river water was warmer than when he came here. He remembered once, years before, he and Audrey had gone away to Wasaga Beach for a weekend in September, and how the water was warmer than the air.

In spite of the heat, there was a little patch of red leaves on one of the big maples. The dryness, someone said, though he'd read somewhere else that it was the change in light that caused the leaves to change colour. He was having trouble finding things to read, almost wished he had those old copies of *National*

Geographic, to see the mountains of Tibet, with smiling Tibetans drinking yak's milk, tribes of Pygmies in the jungles of Africa. What ever happened to the Pygmies? In all the reports of wars and disaster in Africa, there was never any mention of them. As if they never existed at all. One of the tall tales that travellers came back with. Men with heads below their shoulders.

How would he find out if the Pygmies were still there? He wanted to know, supposed that he could drive to Kingston and look them up in the public library, some day when it wasn't so hot. Maybe he should offer Norma a drive to town, though it didn't work out too well the last time he drove her somewhere. Spare Parts. Junk. Carol and Grant had gone up to her store when they were here, and Carol reported that she wasn't rude at all, almost friendly, and when Carman went to the store a few days later to give her a month's rent, she'd pleased him by saying that his daughter was a pretty girl. There might be a library closer than Kingston that would have an encyclopedia. He'd ask her about that.

A day like this, it wasn't hard to imagine the heat of the African jungle, the tiny dark men invisible among the trees. Now there were helicopters overhead, bombs dropping. He put the helicopters out of his mind, thought of the quietness under the high trees, the closeness of the air. Carman closed his eyes and knew that he'd soon be asleep.

Norma was astonished when The Vice-grip arrived at the store offering her a drive to Kingston. A payoff for saying a few days ago that he had a pretty daughter. Well, he did, and the girl had been well-behaved, and Norma had managed for once to be pleasant to him. It emerged that he wanted to go to the library to consult an encyclopedia. Norma offered him a deal. All he had to do was go to the shelves at the back of the shop, and a recent Britannica waited for him. In exchange he could drive her to Aeldred's place. She had some business she wanted to do, and, if the truth be known, and why not, she wanted to look at the old animal, see how he was faring. A vile curiosity.

He wanted to learn about Pygmies, it appeared. Why Pygmies? she said, and he said he just happened to think about them, people will think about the oddest things. So he went to the shelves and took things down and frowned over the books, which told him half of what he wanted to know. Were they still there among the starving millions, and how were they managing? Well, she'd never thought to wonder about that, herself, but she could see it might be of interest to some. Anyway, he found out the names of the tribes and something about their history, and was happy enough to give her a lift. When he asked who Aeldred was, she gave him the purely professional description.

Late in the afternoon, he came back in his big car, and they set out through the baked countryside. It was a little cooler today, but not much. A day to think about the perils of winter. Temperate climate: too hot in the summer, too cold in the winter. Norma remembered the trip to see Spare Parts and speculated on her own ability to sustain a modest level of good manners. When they reached Aeldred's, Carman took a look at the pile of old railway ties, wagon wheels and broken furniture and decided to wait for her where he was, behind the wheel. As she walked up the slope toward the barn, the hot humid air of late afternoon pressed down on her, and she felt her clothes damp with sweat and glued to her skin. She walked out of the bright sunlight and through the wide doors of the barn. The shade of the big building cooled her a little. Old furniture was piled in rows, one thing on top of another, and chairs hung from the ceiling. She looked along a row of chests and into a dark corner where the door of an old tack room stood open, and after a few seconds her eyes adjusted to the darkness and she could see Aeldred sitting on his old bus seat against the stone wall. As she walked toward him, one of his cats, black with a couple of white spots, came out to greet her, the tail straight in the air, the eyes watching her as if assessing how much of her might be edible. Aeldred had a book in his hand, his glasses down on the end of his nose so he could read over the top of them, thighs spread, one hand tucked into the waistband of his trousers. Aeldred could usually be found touching himself somewhere; he liked the feel of flesh, his own if there was nothing else close by. A marmalade cat lay in his lap, a grey one sat on the window sill, and on a pile of straw in the corner, another slept in a heap of kittens. On a table with a broken leg she saw the remains of a meal with flies on it and a bag of shortbread cookies.

'Haven't seen you for a while,' Aeldred said, then looked back at his book, an old one in a dark blue cloth binding. He began to read aloud. 'Mrs Berry is an exceedingly white and lean person. She has thick eyebrows which meet rather dangerously over her nose, which is Grecian, and a small mouth with no lips – a sort of feeble pucker in the face. Under her eyebrows are a pair of enormous eyes, which she is in the habit of turning constantly ceiling-wards.'

'Who wrote all that?'

'Thackeray. From something called *Men's Wives.*

'Was he an expert?'

'Come here and let me look at you.'

The book was set down on the table, and he held out his arms. What he meant was not look but feel, and Norma wasn't at all sure that she was so minded, but she'd always had a weakness for Aeldred, and now she went toward him and he tossed the marmalade cat aside, put his arms around her hips and rubbed his grey beard against her belly and mumbled a little. A smell of cat came from his clothes. A few years back they had the habit of getting together now and then. It had ended when one of Aeldred's women succeeded in getting him to marry her and insisted on fidelity. Norma could have told her that this was a mistake, but she wasn't asked. The marriage didn't last long, but long enough that she got out of the habit of Aeldred and hadn't wanted to start in again. There was something both hypnotic and repulsive about the way his hands were stroking her. Carman had said firmly that he'd stay in the car, but if he were to change his mind and come in, he would be shocked. He looked like a man who might be easily shocked, in spite of all the dark things the police observed.

Norma decided she'd had enough and moved away, and the

marmalade cat came back and began to wind around Aeldred's feet, rubbing against his ankles and purring loudly. Aeldred picked it up.

'Someone said you'd sold your van,' he said.

'The knacker's yard, unhappily.'

'What are you driving?'

'Not. I got a ride with a neighbour.'

She looked at Aeldred's face, the way the thin grey whiskers came out in patches on his cheeks, grew thickly around the mouth, the dark circles around his eyes, and the heavy bags beneath them, the deep wrinkles in his forehead, the grey hair still growing well forward. Ontological Man, he liked to call himself, Pure Being, meaning he was too lazy to get about much, preferred to sit and eat, maybe think a thought now and then, or not, liking to have something warm close by, all in all an indolent fat man without vanity.

'Think I'd cut up satisfactorily,' he said.

'What?'

'You were studying me as if you were planning to sell me to the slaughterhouse.'

'No.'

'Does this neighbour rattle your bones.'

'None of your damned business. Don't presume.'

He shrugged.

'I have no secrets,' he said.

'Do you have any money?' she said.

'Not much.'

'I've got two wood stoves, an old cookstove and an airtight.'

Aeldred made something of a specialty of wood-burning stoves and Quebec heaters. The drive shed beside the barn was full of them. Aeldred looked toward her, then rubbed the back of his neck for a while, pushed his fingers over his face, breathed in and heaved a long sigh.

'You want to sell or trade?'

'I could use an infusion of cash.'

'Did I ever tell you that I was once going to be a dentist?'

'No.'

'I usually tell that story.'

'Is it true?'

'It's a good story.'

Norma said nothing, wanting to force him to reply. She'd got the two stoves for a good price, even with the cost of having Egan McBride and his son-in-law haul them in. Carman's rent was paying for her groceries, but there was a house full of stuff coming up for sale, and she'd like to have the cash on hand to make a prompt offer before the heirs began to have second thoughts.

'What kind of price are we talking about?'

She named a figure. Aeldred stroked the cat, as if trying to feel the shape of its bones. The one in the window jumped to the floor to wind itself around his legs. Aeldred reached down and rubbed it with his hands, moving its loosely hung bones in his grip.

'And I'd have to pick them up, I suppose.'

The cat was stretching itself with pleasure in his hands, but Aeldred's eyes were on Norma, looking her over carefully as if to assess how much weight she'd put on since he'd last lain on top of her and what the effect of the new weight would be. He set the cat aside and reached out for the package of cookies.

'Like a shortbread?'

'No thanks, Aeldred. Never liked them. They have a salty taste.'

'That's the butter,' he said, taking a large bite from one and licking a crumb off his lips with the thick dark red tongue.

'I should never have married that woman,' he said.

'We're talking about money here.'

'You are.'

'You want to think it over, give me a call?' she said.

'I could make you dinner sometime.'

Was it flattering that Aeldred was still interested? Probably more than could be said for that sour old bugger who was sitting waiting in the car, at least as far as she could tell. He looked at her as if she might be a dead fish. A man who'd loved his wife. That's what he was. She was aware that he would be impatient sitting out there in the car, unable to keep still, turning the radio from one station to another then shutting it off.

'I'm going now. You think it over.'

'The price is a little high, but I'll come round and take a look. We might manage something. You could look around while you're here. Maybe we could arrange a trade.'

'I'm looking for cash,' she said. 'You come and check them out.' She turned away, put a foot wrong and hurt her back but tried not to show it. Her face was hot and there was a tingling in her hands and feet. Time to get back to the rocker and close her eyes.

'I should never have married that woman,' Aeldred shouted after her. She stopped and turned in her tracks.

'It was the smartest thing you ever did,' she said. No reason, just bad temper. The shade of the barn failed to cool her now; her clothes were soaked through, and she thought she might faint, but she made the effort, turned back and walked out into the blinding sunlight and got to the car. Carman's dark look was turned toward her as she struggled to get into the seat, used the last of her energy to pull the door shut and put her head back, her eyes closed.

'You all right?' he said.

'It's too damn hot. Too damn hot to live.'

He was starting the car. She kept her eyes closed, running away from it all, though she couldn't have said what that was. The past, perhaps, the smell of Aeldred, the ease with which he'd left her behind for the short-lived marriage, the ease with which he was inviting her back. That was Aeldred: open the package of cookies and eat till they're gone then open another package. All of it together, the heat, the exhaustion, the grim aging appetites, left her empty, unable to even speak. There was nothing to be done.

'You should come down and sit by the water for a while. It's cooler there.'

'Climb in and drown myself. That'd be cold enough.'

He didn't say anything more. She'd been a rude bitch again. Norma knew she should open her eyes, make conversation, but she couldn't do it. Even to open her eyes would take more energy than she possessed, and with them closed she was in her own keeping, untouchable, in a private place as safe as sleep and dreams. The air from the open window blew against her face, and the noise of it against her ears helped. If she could go far enough away, she would find her way to some great joke. The Great Joke of Being. Ontological Man indeed. Consider the lilies of the field was all well enough, but by now he was not much better than a bum, old Aeldred. Sitting in a corner of a barn full of junk, playing with himself. A biological accident that he happened to smell sweet. If he still did. She'd never know. Consider the lilies of the field. Take no thought for the morrow. Be hungry and cold. She could put a sign in the front window of the shop: Spirituality For Sale, Cheap.

She opened her eyes. They were going past one of those bleak hopeless farms built on limestone with a few bare inches of soil over it. By now the owners would have jobs in the city and keep a few cattle as a hobby.

'Damn hard land here,' she said.

'You're alive.'

'Barely.'

'Did you sell him the stoves?'

'What's it to you?'

'I guess you didn't.'

'He's going to come and see them. He'll make me an offer.'

'Will it be good enough?'

'Depends how I'm feeling that day.'

She looked across at him. He gripped the wheel tightly, as if he was strangling it.

'When you were a cop, did you knock people around?'

'Not usually. Didn't need to.'

'Why's that?'

'Most criminals aren't too bright. Even the smart ones screw up eventually.'

They turned at the next crossroads. On the left was a field of hay and on the right was a large woodland, the leaves dark and thick, a wall of green shutting you out.

'There's an old mica mine back in those woods,' she said.

'Mica?'

'All kinds of uses. They used to dig it out of the ground and haul it into town. It was a way of making a few dollars in the winter.'

'Is it all shut down now?'

'Not exactly shut down, just abandoned. Holes in the ground. I have this idea that there must be something to be done with them. Tourists or some damn thing.'

'Some day you should show me.'

'Why?'

'I can be your first tourist. Try it out on me.'

'Then you can start work on the theme park.'

Norma closed her eyes again. She started this trip thinking she liked Aeldred, looking forward to seeing him, but now she hated him, though she had no good reason, no legitimate excuse. He was what he had always been. They turned another corner, and she opened her eyes to find the sun, which was toward setting, was shining straight into them. August heat, but the days were getting shorter already. She looked across the seat at the bulky body of the man with his straight thin hair as he leaned over the wheel.

'When I get home I want to have a little nap,' she said, 'but if you came over later, I'd make a couple of sandwiches.'

'Shall I bring the bottle of rye?'

'You could do that.'

What a stupid idea that was, she thought to herself. She had enough trouble feeding herself.

Carman stood at the edge of the road and listened to the sound of the waterfall, looked at the moths fluttering around the streetlight, and felt the evening air cool on his bare arms. Ghosts watched from the empty hotel. He was a little astonished, pleased with himself, unsettled. He and Norma had drunk too much of the bottle of rye that he'd brought with him, and she had invited him into her bed and he had accepted, not sure whether anything would come of it or whether it would kill him, but they'd managed well enough, and here he was alive and feeling good about it. A bat flew by into the street, a sudden black shape that vanished into the darkness.

She'd made no bones about throwing him out afterward. There had been a little spell of sweetness, but within five minutes of the event, she was starting to get bossy and irritable. He turned his leg the wrong way and got a cramp in the calf and had to parade back and forth naked from one end of her bedroom to the other to try to walk it off, while she dragged a dressing gown off the back of a chair and put it round her. Once the cramp was gone, she handed him his clothes and announced that she didn't want him keeping her up all night, then tromped out of the room and left him to reassemble himself, which he did, looking at the rumpled bed, the pile of books and dirty cups on the table beside it, the jars full of buttons on the chest of drawers, with an old circus poster on the wall behind, clothes hung over chairs and the bedposts. As he got his socks and shoes on, he heard her banging pots and pans in the kitchen, talking aloud. Dressed, he went down the hall and stood in the doorway while she threw things around. When he'd first walked into the apartment, he was shocked at the state of the place, the sink full of dishes, more on the counter and the kitchen table, and Norma had pushed them aside only far enough to make room to slice bread and make a couple of sandwiches. He was just as glad she'd told him to leave. He wouldn't have wanted to see all that in daylight.

As Carman walked back toward the cottage, he realized that he was still a bit drunk. He couldn't remember how much rye they'd gone through. He'd left the bottle on the floor of the living room beside the piece of welded cast iron she called a sculpture. A little breeze came up, shook the leaves over his head, then everything was still. The darkness breathed, and he breathed with it. Alive. Astonishing really. That fat old woman, that crackpot. Pictures on the walls that looked like some mess a kid had made. Dirt in all the corners. He'd gone to use the bathroom once, and the tub was greasy and caked with dirt. There was a metal bar on the wall that helped her get in and out. Bad back. When he was hobbling about with the leg cramp, wincing, she told him to be quiet, that he was in no more pain than she was most of the time. Men were all crybabies. Maybe she was right.

Carman was laughing. The two of them must have been a sight. Himself, he'd grown thick in the middle, lumps over the kidneys, having to slip a pill in his mouth before the act to keep him alive through it all, and she was just this side of obese, and neither of them moved around too gracefully, but they got themselves together and did the job. Carman felt as if he wanted to tell someone, but there was no one to tell. He could imagine Rolly Menard if he got him out of bed in the middle of the night to say he'd just got laid for the first time in years. Too bad Amy Martyrdom had moved. Norma said she liked to talk about these things.

Not that she'd be impressed. What they'd achieved was nothing like the grand opera he'd overheard from the back lawn, but was a very good thing all the same. When he got to the cottage, he walked down toward the river, remembered the pale shadow of Amy's bare body moving through the night. He could think about that without embarrassment now. He'd like to see her there again.

A mosquito flew round his ears, and he slapped at it, without effect. He decided to take the boat out. In the darkness, he missed his footing and got one shoe soaked while he was trying to get the boat untied, but he managed to push it off, and he rowed out into the river and up the first wide section, where he threw the anchor overboard. Its splash was loud in the quietness. When he felt it hit the bottom, he tied it off, and settled himself. By the shore, he could see the dim transient gleam of fireflies. He looked upward, and the dark sky was full of stars. As he sat there, feeling the current of the river pulling his boat against the drag of the anchor, he thought how one night or morning, it would all end. The heart would stop. Sooner or later, and why not? What started must finish.

As he sat there in the night, aching a little, but lightened, wondering what it would be like to have a cigarette again, he thought of all the women in the world. The skinny little hooker with her tight shorts. Amy Martyrdom's big breasts. Back in the cottage, his picture of Audrey sat on the table by the window, impassive and unchanging. Just down the river, beside the waterfall, Norma was settled in the mess of her apartment. He wondered to himself what she was thinking about. He couldn't imagine. Women were different. He doubted that she was thinking how that one act made death a less fearful thing. Right now at least, it did, but he was a little drunk and very surprised and there was no saying what morning would be like.

Somewhere in the night he heard an owl, a sound like a dog barking, and at the edge of the river, the fireflies moved.

Clean the mirrors, Norma. See what you are. No, rather not. Only time is to blame for time. I didn't choose to be old and fat. Not old at least, and it's not clear about the other. A life spent dieting is its own vulgarity. Like Jehovah I am what I am. Should have said no. Most certainly should.

Carman had come by on his way to the grocery store and invited her to come to his cottage where he would barbecue steaks, and she had said yes, and now was in a dither about it, and wondering if she would end up in bed with the man once again, and how much they would need to drink before going at it. That other night, she'd brought it on herself of course, pissed enough to dare and he pissed enough to take the dare, but that was in the past, and the world had spun on its axis a few times since then, sunset, sunrise, the millions at their business. Arteries closed off. Rivers in flood. What she most wanted now was some woman to talk to, wished that Moira would come back from the dead or that Amy Martyrdom was still around, or even that Arthur's Julie would step in the door. Not that she'd tell them about the little adventure, Moira perhaps but not the others, but just to have a woman there would make her less trapped by it. Right? No, not quite that. Hell, she had it wrong, but she had it right as well.

A thing she wanted, and a surprise at that, was to talk to Julie again. Maybe only because Julie had the nerve to come and poke the old bear and take her chances with the teeth and claws. Norma found herself hoping that Arthur stayed with the woman. She might make a human being of him. Well, then, Norma wanted to talk to her, she could pick up the phone, but not so simple, she had no number, didn't even know if she and Arthur lived together, and couldn't find out without asking her son, and she wasn't ready for that. Nothing was what you wanted. After the little adventure with Detective Deshane, she had been unable not to wonder what might come next, and now she'd got what she deserved for wondering, a barbecue by the river and then, and then, and then, and she didn't know if that was what she wanted or what she most didn't want. Nobody deserved to be born to all this. The unborn were safe and holy. It was easier being dead.

A moralizing voice responded, calling for courage. Stuff it, moralizing voice. Enough is enough. Besides he makes me mad, and I'm almost certain to say something rude and bring the evening to an end in disarray. He was another person and other people were too damn much to bear, just being there, just not being you. Notable quotations number 86. Food, though, there would be food, thick red steaks, burnt from the barbecue, bad for the health in every way, nice conventional summer grub, and then they could go out in the boat and watch the moonlight on the water and sing old songs.

She sat down in the rocking chair and gave a couple of good kicks. Now that she'd invited him and he'd invited her, it would be her turn again. Well, he wasn't coming back to the apartment. From what she'd seen, he probably kept the cottage clean, damn him, and next thing he'd be wiping his finger over her tables like a mother-in-law. Censorious. His face was full of disapproval. It was a permanent part of his expression. Men were like that, even Aeldred, who, being dirty, could stand the dirt, would tell her she didn't read widely enough. Widely enough. Blah. She never opened a book any more. Great reader once. Now she stared at the wall, waiting for a crack to open and Entities to flow in from the other side of time. No, Detective Carman Deshane wasn't getting back up the stairs. As a sop to duty, one day, she'd take him off into the woods to see the old mica mines. He'd shown an interest. The bugs in the woods wouldn't be as bad now, after a mostly dry summer.

Maybe he'd have a bright idea about what could be done with the old mines. There must be something.

Red meat and rye whisky. The police force at play. Oh mother, dear mother, come home to us now. Blah. Don't play bingo tonight, mother. Stay home with daddy and me. Blah. Oh hell, bumbling around with whiskied widower was better than being A Victim of Circumstance. Or was it that very thing? How did you know? Deep philosophical questions. The Queen looked down three times from the wall and waited for Norma to answer. The Woman with No Clothes looked back over her shoulder thinking about the answers to all the hard questions and knowing that the perfect health of her big perfect body was the final and eventual answer to all things. At that age being beautiful was a career. At that age Norma didn't look bad. She should have had herself stuffed, like her friend the wolf, whose glass eyes observed her with all the detachment and clarity of a taxidermical god. Two of the smaller animals had sold, to a dusty blonde woman who was a teacher in a free school – an unlikely story, that, Norma thought, as if there still were free schools. However that was, the raccoon and the weasel had gone off to a new life in the big city, and the dusty woman had hankered after the wolf, but Norma, not wanting to lose him, had put the price too high, and now she was tempted to take him upstairs and declare that he was Part of the Establishment.

What she should be doing tonight, instead of going off to some kind of social occasion was getting out her Greek dictionary and learning a little. Become a scholar. Once, she thought she remembered, she had aspired to that, or something like it. She was Good in School. Had a degree, in fact, one of those General BA degrees that could be considered a ladylike accomplishment. Then she took a trip, came back, married Steven, did a little part-time teaching, furnished the house with old furniture that she refinished herself, eventually got knocked up and produced Arthur. As Time Goes By. Remembrance of Things Past. The Recipe for Cookies. How Dumb Can You Get?

As she sat here rocking, little explosions were taking place in the arteries of the brain of the man who once was her husband.

She imagined him sitting at dinner, unable to speak, the panic on his face, Arthur watching him, confused. A transient ischemic attack. She'd read that phrase in a magazine somewhere. She didn't buy magazines, but they came to hand, and she studied things like prostate cancer, preferring the conditions she thought herself least likely to get. What she'd got didn't bear studying, a shapeless set of bad experiences to which they gave one name or another name, the consolation being that it wouldn't kill you. We could just call it old age, she said to the doctor, and had to endure a humourless little lecture on the wonders of medicine in drawing distinctions among the various ways of going down.

She rocked the chair. Aeldred was coming tomorrow to look at the stoves. She had an appointment on the weekend to look at the furniture in the uninhabited house of a dear departed. Intuition told her there would be something good. Aeldred would buy the stoves, she would reinvest the cash and come into possession of good things. Business would boom. Boom. Boom. Boom. Once, for a short spell, she had a bass drum in her stock of rare things.

One thing to be decided was whether to wash herself, at least the smellier bits, and then what to wear. Whatever she wore, she'd probably spill her dinner on it. She was unsettled to realize how much she was looking forward to the first glass of rye. Perhaps the two of them could end up as a pair of muddled and affectionate old topers. No, she didn't want to be one of a pair of anything. As she was thinking about that, the telephone rang.

The great blue heron in the evening twilight. The beak an extension of the thin head and long neck, a sudden and formidable weapon. The body changes shape as the neck unfolds and then extends, the heron still on its long legs, in water that catches the sky's deep blue. A snake armed with a sword. Timeless the world of animals, the predator's patience, stillness going on and on, and then the head plunges into the water and comes out with a fish, turns it, swallows it down, then again the stylized grotesque stillness of the long body in silhouette against the dark mirror, the head like a knife at the end of a whip, the ominous slender potent neck.

Carman watched from his window, fascinated by the bird's perfect concentration as it stood in the shallows on the far side of the river and waited and killed. The light was gradually vanishing into the west, the darkness pouring down over everything, a thick blackness coming out of the east and then in a few hours, morning would come that way again, light creeping over the edge of the world, a grey pallor, then a band of green and gold and pink striking the clouds, and the sun would appear once more.

A boy walking across Camp Hill cemetery in Halifax and then through the Public Gardens, the grass wet with dew, the leaves thick, the air smelling of the sea and of the harbour. What he could remember. That he crossed the Public Gardens and walked past the Lord Nelson Hotel and down Spring Garden Road. While his parents, his older sister, slept. More than once, he got up before anyone in the family, but the summer sun was ahead of him, and the day was bright, the streets still empty except for a milkman and his horse, the wagon stopped at the side of the street, the horse with its tail up, dropping round balls of dung into a steaming heap as it stood waiting, and when the milkman returned and shook the reins, the wagon moved off, the wheels rolling over the fresh turds brown with their speckles of undigested chaff, and once the wagon was gone, sparrows would come to pick it over for something edible. A memory or blend of memories. You knew you must have seen just such a thing, one morning, but you couldn't be certain how many such mornings there were when the boy set off from the little house to walk down to the harbour, where dead fish and driftwood and used safes floated in the water that slopped against the wharves, and there was the big dark shape of an oil tanker on the blue water.

The heron lifted its wings and rose into the darkness and vanished behind the willows. Night and morning, and the seasons passed, and in winter, the river would run through fields covered with snow, black and shining among the white fields. He wondered if it would ever freeze over. The current was strong. When he sat in the boat fishing, he could feel it pulling against the anchor. It would be interesting to know if the river froze. He didn't know what he was going to do in the fall. He could stay on here for a month or so after Labour Day, but the place would be too cold after that. It had no foundation and wasn't winterized like the cottage next door. Which was still empty. Norma said Amy had a lease for another six months.

Norma was in Toronto for a funeral. It was just before she came down to the cottage for steaks that she heard her former husband had died of a stroke. She didn't mention it to Carman until after she'd had a couple of drinks. He could have said she was in a strange state of mind that night, except she always was, so far as he could see. Here's to the night, she kept saying as she drank. Here's to the night and the darkness. He thought perhaps she wouldn't want to go to bed with him, but she was eager, in a defiant kind of way; then he'd hardly caught his breath when she was back up on her feet, dressing in the dark, vanishing out the door.

That boy walked through Halifax on a summer morning, making his way down to the harbour to dream of ships. Time was he went to sea and saw a war. Came back and joined the police. Even then the world was simple. They pursued and entrapped queers, hanged murderers. Criminals knew what they were and expected what they got. Gradually it got to be something else, until it wasn't clear who was on your side and who wasn't, and then suddenly you woke in the morning with aches and pains. One morning in the cemetery he saw a couple asleep under one of the bushes, their arms round each other, their faces empty, and he thought that they must have been there all night, and he was frightened for a second that they might be dead. He looked at them, the woman's round face, the man's sandpapery whiskers, wondered where they would go when they woke up, and then he walked on, and at the corner of Barrington Street there was an old woman staring up into one of the trees, as if she might find a great bird or an angel waiting for her, bringing her a message.

Norma sat in her rocking chair, and the universe went on about its business. Summer at its peak, ready to end. In Antarctica, it was the dead of winter, and the wind howled over the mountains and the endless expanses of ice. It was the coldest place in the world and its seasons were upside down. So they said. Yesterday, she had sold several pieces of furniture to a couple who were furnishing a cottage, and had got a good price for a mahogany sideboard picked up the week before. Last night as she lay in bed, a breeze touched her, and she thought it was the first hint of fall.

Steven was still dead. Dutiful for once, she had gone to Toronto to stand up and bear witness with the man's only son, at a brief and awkward moment in the funeral home, everything in the charge of some non-denominational cleric who was a friend of somebody's friend. The bimbo sent flowers. God, it was all so awful. Norma did her best to be a good conventional person, not to embarrass Arthur by farting or tripping or saying something rotten, and perhaps she'd succeeded, trying to think kind thoughts about Steven. To imagine that the years they'd spent together were good, and maybe they were, some of them. She remembered their marriage ceremony. That was awful too. He was a good fuck most of the time. He earned a living. What else was there to marriage?

What did the Antarctic penguins do in winter? Did they still parade around in their comical fashion or did they swim north to someplace a little warmer? Life was full of large questions. If you are an Antarctic penguin, how cold is too cold? Why are penguins funny? Do they see the joke? Oh Coldest Antarctica. The Mountains of the South Pole. The End of the Known World. Like Carman pursuing his Pygmies, she could look it up.

When it was over, they all went back to Arthur's apartment near Davisville and Mount Pleasant. Julie, it appeared, had a place of her own, farther east. Norma took herself for a walk a little way down Mount Pleasant, looking in the windows of restaurants and florists and furniture stores, all very pleasant, Mount Pleasant, and she wept a few tears, for herself most likely, maybe for Steven, long gone as he was, and then she went back to the apartment, looked out the windows at the lights of the endless city, let Arthur and Julie take her out to dinner at an expensive restaurant all done in black and silver and selling fish things and strange vegetables, and after a sleepless night on a bed unfolded from a couch, she got into Julie's car and was driven back. They talked a little during the trip, not much, and when they arrived, the river was still running, the waterfall still falling. As she climbed out of the car, Norma saw a boat on the water, Carman fishing. Norma offered to have Julie overnight, and meant the invitation, wanted her to stay, but she said she had to be at work early the next morning and left.

She could understand the people who had a dozen children. Never any peace, but life was compelled, and surely there were not these moments when the rocking chair refused to rock, and it was hard to remember why. She kicked out her legs. One decision had been made. She was going to buy a car, some kind of efficient little thing. Cash her RRSP and to hell with old age. Mobility was needed, at least until she settled in her little seniors' apartment with the cable TV and gave her soul to the airwaves.

She tried to remember Steven's face and wasn't sure she could. Served him right. She could remember his private parts, what he was proudest of, after all, like most men. She wondered what the bimbo brought to mind from her youthful adventure. One dick among many. After Norma bought her car, she would drive to Kingston and look at all the places she had lived, mostly places that she and Steven had lived together. That was the last thought he'd get from her. In fact, until Arthur turned up with his new girl she had largely succeeded in putting him out of her mind. That was harder with the dead. The living were moving on, and you could never imagine what they might be up to so you ignored them. The dead had nothing but their past, and so they were complete and persisted in being what they were. Gone, they were harder to forget. Even stupidity took on a certain mute perfection.

Norma was thinking. Sitting and rocking and thinking. Though of a highly variable temperament, she was at the moment in the grip of a certain serenity. Or was it inertia? Through the front window of the store, she could see two couples in holiday garb, examining her things and engaging in discussion. They opened the door. One of the women had the look of someone who has already made up her mind.

Carman tripped over a small outcropping of rock and nearly went sprawling. Norma stopped, stared at him with a look on her face that made him want to knock her down.

'You'd want to watch where you're going.'

'I'll do that.'

If he said anything more he'd find he was getting mad, and if he got mad, he'd get madder. All the way along the road since they'd left her store she'd picked at his driving, like a child picking at a sore, as if she was determined to start a fight over something. A mosquito landed on his neck. He started to walk faster. Her breath came heavily from just behind him.

'What's your damn hurry?'

'The woods are full of bugs.'

'I haven't seen any.'

'I have.'

'They must be attracted to your sweetness.'

He didn't answer. The whole outing was ridiculous. He didn't care about the damned old mica mines, however determined she was to get there. She should get a car of her own instead of expecting him to drive her all over the countryside. He watched where he was walking to avoid tripping again. They were following some sort of old road, a logging road maybe, that wound through the rock of the Shield and the second-growth bush – maple and beech and a few birches, here and there a tall spruce. It wasn't a hot day, but he was sweating from the exercise, and Norma was puffing more heavily behind him. He didn't look back. A hundred years before, men had come in here and logged it. Had the road been cut to take the mica out? A truck or tractor must drive in now and then or it would have been completely overgrown.

Something was waiting for you in the woods, though you never knew what it was. Even that little bush behind the motel. The fish, the memory of an old crime in the air. Here it was the hard men leading hard lives, who had given themselves to this cold rocky place and broken or not broken. Everyone broke eventually. He felt the pocket of his jacket to make sure he had the nitroglycerin pills. Magic against sudden death.

Norma spoke from behind him.

'I don't know if you're trying to kill yourself or me,' she said, 'but either way, slow down.'

Her voice was hoarse because she was short of breath. He stopped and looked back. Her face was pale.

'Is it much farther?'

'I can't quite remember. I'll recognize it when I get there. Remains of an old shed by the road and a path off to the left.'

'You want to sit down and rest?'

'I'm not such a damn cripple as that.'

He started walking again. A red squirrel chattered at them. A jay screamed. The old hard lives whispered behind the trees, invisible among leaves and branches.

'There's the shed just up there.'

It wasn't a shed any more but a pile of old grey boards rotting away. Carman doggedly put one foot in front of the other. He thought he remembered saying he wanted to come here, but right now he couldn't think why he'd had such an idea. They reached the shed and Norma said that just beyond it they should go to the left, and when they did they were in a bit of a clearing, with a slope down at the far side, and a couple of piles of rock. The ground was uneven, and under his feet the earth was soft and slippery, he saw that the ground was covered with glittering fragments of mica. Norma was going on ahead of him and he bent and picked up a couple of pieces of the odd substance.

She was talking, more to herself than to him. There was a scrabbling noise, a gasp, and she was gone. He stared, as if this might be some kind of childish trick and in a moment he would see her peeking at him from behind a tree. The woods were silent except for the wind in the leaves and the sound of a jay, and already he was moving carefully to where he had last seen her. The edges of the deep hole were thick with fallen leaves, and when he looked down, he saw her in the water, below steep sides of rock and earth. The edges were slippery with fragments of mica. The water must have flowed into the open pit where the mica had been dug. He looked around him again, as if there might be someone to help. He was a city cop. You always had a radio, a phone. If you went into the burning building, you knew that help was on its way.

By now he was sitting on the edge of the pit. It was perhaps eight feet down to where she was, and if he slipped into the water, he'd never get out. He eased his body over the edge, his legs out to catch the sides and slow his descent as he slid down. The rocks scraped him and he could feel his hands being torn, but by lying flat against the slope, he used the drag of his body and clothes against gravity and managed to stop himself at the edge of the water. One leg went in, but his right foot was on a small rock ledge, and he anchored his weight there. He could see her body in the dark water just under the surface where three yellow leaves floated, and there was a shimmer of reflection of the sky. He reached in and got hold of something and pulled. He realized that he was holding her by the hair, but he didn't dare change his grip or he'd drop her. He had her face out of the water. There was a nasty wound on one side of her head, a little blood, and she must have been knocked unconscious as she fell. As far as he could tell, she was breathing, but it didn't seem possible to get her out of here.

His heart was pounding, and he could feel the familiar pain and tightness in his chest. They could both die down here. He looked up, to see how far he had to lift her, and at the edges of the hole he could see little glittering fragments of the mica. He was holding Norma out of the water with his left arm, and it was starting to ache. He got his right hand into the pocket of his jacket, managed to get out two pills and put them under his tongue. A little magic to help him along. Beside him, there was a place where the slope of the old excavation was a little less steep, and he reached down, got his other hand on a piece of her clothing and leaned toward that side. It took all his strength, but he got her head and shoulders out of the water; he knew if he let go, she'd slide back in. For a moment, he stayed still, bent over the round face with its roll of fat beneath the chin, but she was breathing slowly, blood spreading from the wound, the eyes closed, for once not staring at him.

'You really are a pain in the ass, Norma,' he said.

He tried to think, to make a plan. He couldn't lift her out of the hole. Even young and healthy he couldn't have done that. The only hope was to get out himself, which would be hard enough, and to pull her out. With what? Bent over, he put one knee on her shoulder and pressed down, to hold the inert body in place against the slope, and with his hands free, he took off his belt. Then, pushing her about unrespectfully, manhandling her heavy breasts, he managed to work the belt around the body and under her arms and to buckle it. It gave him a kind of handle, and using it to move her, he managed to get himself a few inches higher and get her body a little further out of the water. Her hips were on the ledge, with the legs dangling, but now he could let her lie there for a second and rest his arms. Once more he examined the old digging. A little above him a tree root as thick as his wrist grew out of the earth. He reached up and took hold of it. It looked solid, and he reached up, took it with his right hand and pulled. He let his weight drag on it, and it held. That might be enough to get him back out, but he didn't dare leave her. Awkwardly, nearly losing his balance and falling into the water himself, he took off his trousers. He put the wallet and keys in his jacket pocket, then tied one leg of the trousers around the belt he'd strapped below Norma's arms. He pulled on it, hard and dragged her a little further away from the water, then he reached up and tied the other end round the piece of root. If she came to and struggled, would she plunge herself back into the water? He didn't know, but he knew that he was never going to get her out of here on his own.

He stood for thirty seconds and breathed as slowly and calmly as he could.

'Norma,' he said loudly and touched her face.

The eyes in their pouches of skin opened for a second.

'You fell into an old mine,' he said. 'I can't get you out, but you're tied so you can't slip in again. You'll have to wait here while I go for help. Do you understand?'

Her eyes opened and then closed and she lay inert, but she was still breathing, and when he checked the pulse in her neck, it was steady. He looked up and wondered if he could get himself out. Best to go very slowly. The root would hold his weight, if he could get his foot on it, and then he might be able to reach out of the hole. He saw a couple of soft spots just above his feet, where the ground was soft and full of bits of mica, and he tried kicking his toes into one of them, and he managed to get a toe hold in one, then in the other. Within a few minutes, he was standing on the root. There was pain in his chest, and he was having trouble getting his breath now, and for a long time he stood there and gathered his strength. He heard Norma moaning a little and he spoke to her, repeating his reassurances, telling her to wait. If he could just stay alive long enough to get to the road, it would be all right. Someone would come.

His fingers were searching just over the edge of the hole for something he could hold to pull himself out. He tore at grass, but it came loose and dirt fell into his face. There was nothing. Once more he kicked into the dirt until he had a toehold, and he found a rock just above his head where his fingers got a little purchase. He levered himself up, though he hated to step away from the stability of the thick root, but now he got his left hand farther out and found a bush he could grip, and it held his weight while he scrabbled up and got an elbow over the edge. He was kicking dirt back down onto the woman below, but there was no help for it. Awkwardly he dragged himself over the top, then lay on the ground panting until he could get to his feet and start back through the woods, the way they'd come. Close to his face, he saw an ant holding something in its mandibles as its thin legs carried it over a dead leaf. He pushed himself up.

Dirty-faced, his shirt-tails hanging over his underpants, he started to walk as fast as he dared through the woods. Sunlight in the leaves made it look like a scene from a calendar. Great outcroppings of rock were covered with lichen. He was still breathing hard, and his whole body was aching. He thought he'd never been so tired. He got out a couple more pills and took them. As he walked, he checked the pockets of his jacket. The cars keys were still there; if need be, he'd drive to a neighbour's house. He thought of Norma coming to consciousness and discovering herself trussed in a belt and tied to a root with a pair of trousers. She wasn't a stupid woman. She'd figure it out and wait. So he hoped. Or she'd kill herself out of sheer bad temper.

He was in the grass of the overgrown field that led to the road, and through the bushes at the edge of the road, he could see his car. He tried to remember where they'd passed the nearest house, couldn't, but when he got to the road, he heard a car engine, and aware that he looked ridiculous, standing in his underpants, wet and ruinous, he summoned up his old police dignity, stepped into the middle of the road and held up his hand to stop whatever was coming. Well, Norma, he said to himself, when he saw the vehicle approaching, you were born with a horseshoe up your ass. It was two men in a four-by-four. The driver had a funny look on his face as Carman came up to the door, but before he'd heard half the story, he had his friend out opening the wire gate that led to the road through the woods, and in a minute, Carman was in the back seat, and they were bouncing through the woods to the place he'd left Norma.

Carman just sat leaning against a tree and watched them while they got her up. Even with the two of them, the vehicle, and chains, it wasn't easy, and she got bumped a little, but within fifteen minutes she was out. Carman just sat, exhausted. One man was tall and one was short and they moved around with a certain frantic efficiency. Carman watched as if it made sense, but he was helpless and a long way off. The men put her in the four-by-four, and the two of them were about to set off to drive her to the hospital in town. They assumed Carman was coming with them, that he'd want to stay with her, but Carman had rescued his trousers, what was left of them, and all he wanted was for them to drop him off at his car, even though he wasn't sure whether he could drive. He was no help to anyone now. The driver – his name was Larry or Harry or Garry – offered to drive Carman home after they got Norma seen to, but he refused. He'd had enough. When he saw them drive away, he opened the door to drive himself home but he was starting to shiver, and he didn't think he could drive yet, so he got in the back seat and curled up there, pulled a blanket over himself and waited for the shivering to go away. He wasn't sure that he shouldn't check himself into the hospital as well, but he wasn't going to do that. That would kill him for sure. His chest hurt, and he felt in his pocket for a pill, wondered if he'd taken too many. After a while, the shaking eased a little, and he fell asleep, and by the time he woke up, the afternoon sun bright in his eyes, he felt as if he could drive back to the cottage and get himself cleaned up, take his ration of pills and pour a good-sized shot of rye.

Norma tried to move in the narrow hospital bed, but the weight of the cast kept her still. She lay in the darkness of her room and watched as Doctor Life and Doctor Death went softly past along the hallway. She'd asked the nurses to leave the door open for the night, terrified of being trapped in here. About as mobile as a beached whale with this cast on and her back half useless. In the other bed, her roommate, a woman who'd fallen off a roof, snored softly. She hadn't explained to Norma how she got on the roof to begin with. Now and then Nurse Pain would go by in one direction, Nurse Grief in the other. A machine beeped, or an announcement would be heard on the hospital PA. Once she had been told the code for a cardiac emergency. Code 99, was that it? The sudden drama beloved of television. Danger and resurrection. Most of the time Doctor Life and Doctor Death went about their slow business of postponement. Medicine was the science of postponement.

Norma's broken head ached, as did her deteriorated back and broken leg, but she wouldn't call for Nurse Pain and ask for something. Tomorrow she would be home and could take an occasional aspirin from her little stock of medicaments. Mostly her medicine cupboard was full of the soap and toiletries that Moira used to give her for Christmas and which she never used up. That and two cans of baked beans. She had no idea how the baked beans had got there. One day she looked, and there they were, and she couldn't bring herself to take them out. Surely baked beans could cure something.

Her last visit to The Vice-grip at her cottage, she'd taken a look in his medicine cabinet after using the toilet. He had all colours and shapes of prescription drugs. Must be in terrible shape. She didn't want him dying on her hands. She supposed she ought to feel gratitude to him for dragging her out of that hole, but it came hard. She'd never have fallen in if he hadn't made her so mad that she was blinded by irritation. Driving like a maniac, getting in a snit when she mentioned it, then trying to defeat her by walking so fast and whining about the bugs. No wonder his wife had died. Only way to get away from him. He'd been to see her this afternoon and offered to pick her up when she was released in the morning. She'd agreed to that though she didn't want to. What she should have done was get Aeldred to come for her in the truck. Set her up in the back of it in an old stuffed chair. Better than building up a debt of gratitude. Aeldred had given her the eye the day he'd come to get the stoves. Easier to deal with him, lazy and disreputable as he was. Tried to cheat her on the stoves, but she didn't let him.

She hadn't told Arthur she was in here. In fact there was no need for them to keep her once they'd bandaged her head and put a cast on her leg and probed and pinched a few places to make sure she was alive. They wanted her to stay for observation, but she didn't think anyone had observed much. Check vital signs, offer bad food, say good night. When she got home she'd write Arthur a letter and tell him about the adventure. Not that she could remember much. Falling, cold, being trussed up, The Vice-grip talking to her, then those two yahoos – Garry and Paul, why did she remember their names? – hauling her out, a lot of shouting and grinding of motors, chains. Attached a chain to her and just let the little truck drag her to the surface, was that it? Maybe not. It seemed to her that one of them was down the hole with her. By then she was aware she was soaking wet, and the cold went all the way through her bones. As they drove to town, they kept her wrapped in a blanket and Paul told jokes to encourage her. They were bad jokes. Country jokes.

Apparently she'd been underwater when Carman got hold of

her. She couldn't remember any of that. Feet in the water maybe. A wonder she hadn't caught pneumonia, but apart from the bangs and bruises she was in working order. Doctor Life and Doctor Death passed by in white coats. What were they doing here in the middle of the night? Was someone dying? Steven had died. And Moira. Funny thing to be dead. It was her belief that anger would keep her going for some while yet. Rage will keep you forever young. Acting youthful too: she'd been performing the act of generation, though nothing would be generated, and a damn good thing too. It was too late for the dozen children now. She had what she was going to get.

If she ever got out of this cast and mobile she might be tempted to do it again, a pleasant thing, but she wouldn't have him around in the morning to hear her moans and groans, to see the laborious struggle to get her out of bed and standing. A little passing warmth was enough. A night act done in the night.

One of the nurses had got her clothes washed and dried so she'd have something to go home in. Something else to be grateful about. Norma had been as unctuous as she could manage. It was a kindness, but she preferred not to need kindnesses. Never need anything. Only possible if you were richer than she'd ever be.

One of the doctors passed the door on his soft silent shoes. Was it Doctor Life or Doctor Death? She wasn't sure she could tell them apart.

At ten o'clock, he drove up to the front of the hospital, and saw the nurse push the wheelchair through the automatic doors. Norma's leg in its heavy cast stuck out in front of the chair, and the bandage on her forehead, the black eye and bruising down one side of her face made her look like two people, one whole, one damaged. She was staring aggressively at the cars, but when he pulled up, she looked away. He got out and waved to the nurse who pushed the wheelchair over while he opened the passenger door.

'Stupid business,' Norma said, 'pushing me out here in a wheelchair like some kind of cripple.'

'It's a hospital rule,' the nurse said. 'Once I put you in the car, you're on your own.'

'Give Carman another chance to kill me. It was him knocked me down the mine shaft, you know. Terrible bad temper.'

Carman ignored that. The nurse, who was a small woman, from the Philippines he would have guessed, looked at him as if assessing whether that might be true.

'You're Norma's husband,' she said.

'He certainly is not,' Norma said.

'A neighbour,' Carman said.

'Tenant. On a temporary basis.'

The nurse had Norma on her feet, and was about to help her into the car.

'I think the back seat would be better,' she said. 'More room for the cast.'

'Yes,' Norma said. 'Make it that much harder for Carman to finish me off.'

Carman closed the passenger door and opened the other one, and the two women got Norma in, sitting sideways, with the cast stretched across the seat. Norma gave a royal wave to the nurse who closed the door, smiled at Carman and pushed the wheelchair back into the building. Carman got into the driver's seat.

'Let's get the old girl out of here,' Norma said.

Carman pulled out of the driveway and drove down to the lakeshore.

'Why are you going this way?'

'Because it's the way I want to go.'

'It's the longest way.'

'It's the way I want to go.'

Norma leaned over so she could see herself in the rear-view mirror.

'What a mess,' she said. 'I look even worse than usual.'

Two sailboats moved over the smooth water of the lake, the white curve of their sails outlined against the blue water and blue sky. Closer to shore, a figure in a wetsuit was skimming across the water on a sailboard.

'Are the customers lined up at the door?' she said.

'Weren't when I left this morning.'

'No, I guess not.'

The road turned away from the water, and the sailboats disappeared.

'I suppose I should thank you,' Norma said. 'For saving my life.'

'You're welcome. But don't do it again.'

'Why not? A bit of excitement. Adventure.'

'It damned near killed me getting you out of that water.'

'Such a fat woman.'

'That's all right so long as I don't have to haul you out of any more holes.'

'How did you do it?'

'I'm not sure I remember. Ask me after I've had a couple of drinks.'

The car moved through traffic, going toward the highway that would take them back out into the country.

'You're going to have trouble with the stairs,' he said. 'With that cast on.'

'I have trouble with the stairs without the cast.'

'We can get you up there, but you'll never get back down.'

'I suppose I could close the place.'

'I'll come over and run the shop if you like. Sit in the rocking chair for a few hours. That's all you do, isn't it?'

'I think a lot. It's the thinking that's the hard part.'

'You can do that upstairs. If anyone comes in, I can likely find something rude to say. It will be just the same as if you were there.'

'I'm never rude to customers.'

'You were rude to me.'

'That's you. You looked like a murderer.'

'Well, I'm not.'

'Anyway, it's Labour Day next week.'

'I thought I might stay on.'

Norma looked at herself in the rear-view mirror again, made a face and slumped back in the seat.

'So you're going to be around for a while yet,' she said.

'A while.'

'What are you going to do when it gets cold?'

'I called Amy and arranged to sublet the other cottage for a few months. It's winterized.'

'You did that?'

'Yes.'

Norma said nothing. Then she made some noises as if she were talking, but not opening her mouth. Then silence. They drove through the last of the suburbs and into the countryside. The grass was dry, full of wildflowers. Carman felt a little dizzy and was having trouble concentrating on the road. He'd be glad when the trip was over.

'So you're going to spend the winter down there by the river.'

'Looks like it.'

'I expect you'll regret it.'

'I might or I might not.'

'Why are you staying?'

'Same reason I drove along the lakeshore. Because I want to.'

'Damn wilful man.'

'Yes.'

My thanks to Mabel Corlett for guiding me to the mica mines, many years ago, when I was planning an altogether different book.

JUDY GAUDET

Born in Ontario, David Helwig attended the University of Toronto and the University of Liverpool. He taught at Queen's University, worked in summer stock, was literary manager of CBC Television Drama and has done a wide range of freelance writing. He is the author of more than twenty books. His most recent works are a novella, *The Stand-In* (The Porcupine's Quill, 2002), and a long poem, *The Year One* (Gaspereau Press, 2004).

David Helwig currently lives on Prince Edward Island.

Also by David Helwig

The Stand-In, Porcupine's Quill

The Year One, Gaspereau

The Time of Her Life, Goose Lane

Living Here, Oberon

A Note on the Type

Giambattista Bodoni (1740–1813) was known as the King of Printers. The Bodoni font he created in 1767 displaced the earlier Old Face and Transitional styles and eventually became one of the most popular typefaces until it fell from favour in the mid-nineteenth century. Bauer Bodoni was introduced in 1926 by the Bauer type foundry of Frankfurt, Germany. Bauer Bodoni was designed by Heinrich Jost (1889–1949) who was the artistic director of the foundry from 1822 to 1948.